To Each His Own

Also by the author:

Lady of Spain

A Reluctant Hero

Redemption

The Girl Who Made Good in America

The Americanization of Sarah Gall

Imagine All the People

The Rhythm of Life

To Each His Own

James G Dow

Cover Design and typeset by BookPOD
Front cover image iStockPhoto

A Catalogue-in-Publication is available from
the National Library of Australia.

ISBN: 978-0-6484083-4-5 (pbk)
eISBN: 978-0-6484083-5-2

Foreword

The rank is but the guinea stamp.
The man's the gold for a' that.

Robert Burns

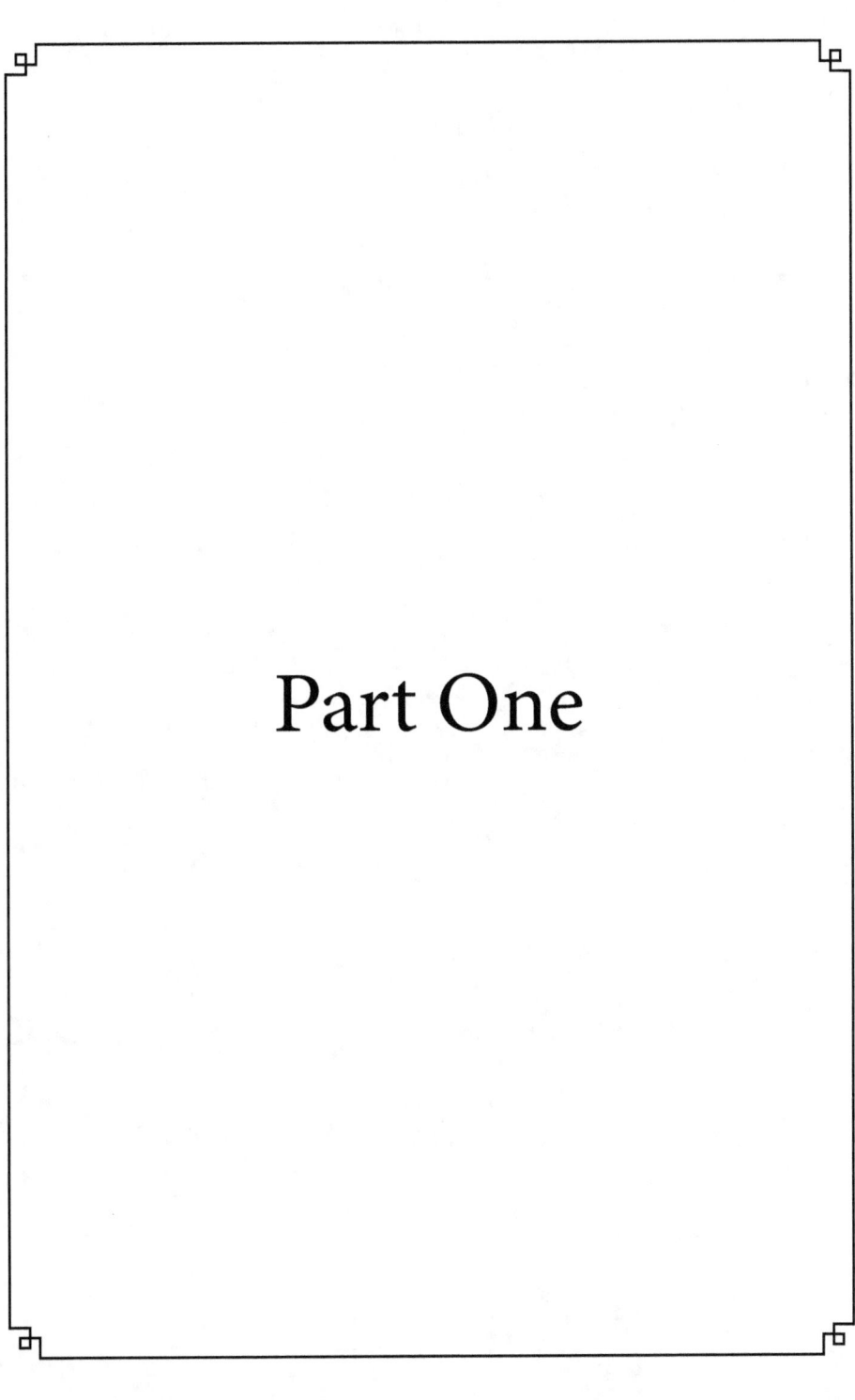

Part One

Chapter 1

1930

Starvation will loom
Amid economic gloom

"There's no' a scrap o' food in the place. The bairns are away to school on empty bellies." She burst into tears. "I tell ye, Jock, I'm at ma wit's end."

"Aye, I know what you're goin' through, lass. I've just had a run o' bad luck but I get paid today. We'll have food on the table tonight."

"Oh, Jock, your wages won't be enough to fix our problems. The rent's way overdue. The man said we'd be on the street if we get further behind."

"Look, Jeannie, I'll go and talk to the landlord ... get him to give us a wee bit more time to get ourselves sorted."

"Mr Pottinger, I've come to ask a wee favour on behalf of ma wife and weans ... just a few weeks to catch up on the rent."

"Mr MacDonald, I've been carrying you for months already, not weeks. I'm not made of money ... I've got creditors who demand payment on the dot from me."

"But I'm tryin' ma best, Mr Pottinger ... things will swing ma way in a wee while."

"I wish I could believe you, Mr MacDonald, but everyone in town knows that you have a gambling problem. It's your fault that your wife can't make ends meet. I'm sorry ... you'll have to come up with rent arrears or you'll be in the hands of the bailiff."

"Surely, you wouldn't chuck ma bairns oot, Mr Pottinger?"

"Not me ... you're the culprit here."

Jock MacDonald left Mr Pottinger's office in a dark mood. He had no idea what else he could do. However, first things first ... he was on the middle shift at Twechar pit, 10am till 6pm. Something might turn up today. Jeannie will likely get some food on tick from Papa Joe Lennox. His shop always does well and he's a kindly soul. Aye, she'll be all right today.

Chapter 2

Overcoming shame, she once more deigns
To beg for food to feed her weans

*J*eannie had no faith in her husband's promises. He'd led her down
that path too often. A while back, she got a basket of groceries on
credit from Papa Joe. She had never repaid that debt and now she'd have to
go and beg for some more tick. If he threw her out, she couldn't blame him.
However, she sensed that Papa Joe had feelings for her, although he was
married. Now, she'd have to do something really embarrassing. Suddenly,
she remembered that about six months ago, his wife had passed away,
shortly after Jeannie had received the groceries. Jeannie hadn't been back
in his shop since then because she never had the money to repay him.

She wheeled the bairn in the pram up to Papa Joe's store just before it
closed for lunch. With her heart in her mouth, she quietly entered. Joe saw
her and locked the front door, switching the sign to 'Closed for lunch'.

"Hello, Jean ... it's lovely to see you."

"Oh, Mr Lennox, I ..."

"Call me Joe, Jean. Look, I can see you need help. The bairn's crying ...
is she hungry, lass?" Without waiting for an answer, he lifted the bairn out
of the pram. "When did you last feed her, Jean?"

"Last night, Joe, she finished the last o' the bottle then."

"So, you're not breastfeeding her, lass?"

"No, I dried up a coupla weeks ago."

"I'm not surprised, Jean ... you look as if you could do with a feed yourself."

"Oh, Joe, don't bother aboot me ... can ye fill the wean's bottle?"

"I can, but the wee lass has a rash ... how long has she had that?"

"Oh, about a week, Joe. I'll have to take her to the doctor but I haven't got the cash to pay him."

"Jean, I have a niece over in Lenzie with a bairn who had the same problem. Her husband works with the Department of Health as a nutritionist. He ran some tests and discovered his daughter was allergic to cow's milk. I suspect your bairn is the same."

"Well, Joe, I've got to feed her somethin'. What does your niece do?"

"She gives her bairn soylac. I've got it in stock. Quite a few women in the town use it. The problem is fairly common these days."

Jeannie handed him the baby's bottle and Joe filled it with soylac. He heated it gently and handed it to Jeannie. Full of doubts about this soy stuff, she cradled the bairn in her arms and offered her the bottle. The wee lassie gulped it down greedily. Jeannie put her over her shoulder and burped her. The bairn was quiet as her mother laid her in the pram. She smiled and fell asleep.

"Oh, Joe, I don't know how to thank ye," said Jeannie, bursting into tears. She hugged Joe close. "How can I ever repay you for that?"

"Well, for a start, you can join me for lunch. Come on, lass, you're starving."

Jeannie dried her eyes and nodded.

He sat her down at his kitchen table and heated up a pot of soup. As he handed her a bowl of the steaming broth, he said, "Get that into you, lass. That'll stick to your ribs."

He made some toast and joined her at the table. They ate in silence until she said, "Joe, that was really good but ..."

"... I know what you're going to say, so there's no need to say it. You have nothing at home for the two boys when they come home from school ... right?"

She nodded, dismally and whispered, "That's true."

"Look, let's fill your basket with tatties, lentils, barley, carrots, turnips ... enough to make soup for three days."

She was crying again, "How can I ever pay ye back, Joe?"

"Don't worry about that, lass. I can't see you and the bairns going hungry. You'll pay me some day. Now, leave by the back lane and here's a couple of loaves and a few bottles of soylac. That seems to have done the trick and I'm sure that rash will clear up quick smart. Now, off ye go and don't be a stranger ... you must know I'm fond of you, Jean."

Chapter 3

The gambler's on a slippery slope,
Out of luck and out of hope

As Jock MacDonald descended in the cage with the other miners, his thoughts were far removed from the task at hand. He was having pangs of conscience and was now determined that his gambling days were behind him. The trouble was that his financial problems were real and immediate and, unless some miracle occurred, he had no idea how to solve them.

The cage decelerated and reached bottom with a thud, rousing Jock from his reverie. Now, he was all business as he strode to the coal seam to which he and Charlie Feeney were assigned. The seam was only three feet high but wide enough for two men to work side by side. They had to kneel to swing their picks and it was hard work. With all his faults, Jock MacDonald had always been a conscientious worker and that concentrated his mind on the job, driving his private problems into the background. Charlie, occasionally, had to ask Jock to take it easy, to let him keep abreast.

After three hours, Charlie called for a halt. "Come on, Jock, let's fill a couple of bogeys before we eat."

Jock reluctantly laid down his pick and shovelled the coal they'd dug into the bogeys. The two then sat down and Charlie opened his piecebox, taking out a hefty cheese sandwich. "Where's your piecebox, Jock?"

"Och, I forgot to bring it ... anyway, I'm no' hungry. I'll just have a rest."

"Oh, for Christ's sake, Jock, ye cannae work a whole shift on an empty stomach. Come on, man, I've got plenty ... here, have a hunk o' bread and cheese."

Jock hesitatingly accepted the sandwich and the two men ate in silence. As soon as Jock finished eating, he stood and lifted his pick. Charlie could see that his workmate was restless and anxious to get started again. Charlie knew that they would achieve their quota today without having to panic. Nevertheless, he rose and joined his mate at the coal face without objection.

The pair worked steadily until four o'clock when Jock had pulled ahead again. "Jock, have a breather for five minutes so that I can catch up. We're not all supermen, laddie."

Jock smiled and said, "OK, Charlie, I need to take a leak anyway." He strolled back and relieved himself at the side of the tunnel. As he turned to resume work, there was a crash as the tunnel roof caved in across the seam. He rushed back and saw that Charlie's head and upper body were covered in rubble but his hips and legs were free. Furiously, Jock began to clear the rocky rubble from Charlie's body. Fortunately, there were no excessively heavy rocks but twenty minutes elapsed before he managed to drag his mate away from the seam. He checked to see if Charlie was still alive. He was breathing and his pulse was strong and steady but he was unconscious. Jock lifted his mate onto the leading bogey and pushed it towards the coal collection elevator. This took about five minutes. When he got to the cage, he picked up the phone.

"What's up?" said the winding engineman.

"This is Jock MacDonald. There's been a cave-in at our seam. I've got Charlie Feeney in a bogey ... he's unconscious. Get us up and call an ambulance as well."

Within minutes, Jock and the bogey surfaced. Charlie was placed on a stretcher and covered with a blanket, awaiting the ambulance. Charlie regained consciousness as they were putting him in the ambulance, which would transport him to the Glasgow Royal Infirmary.

The mine manager called Jock up to his office to get the details straight from the horse's mouth, as it were. Jock told him exactly what had happened, without embellishment.

"You did well, MacDonald. The engineer and his squad are already down there, shoring up the roof. You can go to the pay clerk and pick up your wages. There will be a bit extra for you this week."

Jock went straight to Eddie Feeney's office. Eddie was the pay clerk and Charlie Feeney's older brother. "Hello, Eddie, the manager sent me over to pick up ma pay packet."

"Here ye are, Jock. He's just about doubled your wages this week."

"I dunno why, Eddie. I just did what any miner woulda done."

"I know that, Jock, but the boss man has never worked at the coal face so he's not aware of your unwritten law. Charlie knows the rules so he won't be thankin' ye for savin' his life."

"I know that, Eddie ... I mean, it might be him savin' me next week. Still, I won't be turnin' up ma nose at the extra cash."

"Well, Jock, I'm not a miner either so I'm grateful for what ye did. I believe you like to have a bet ... is that right?"

"I used to but I can't afford to lose any more money, Eddie. Why do ye ask?"

"My mate, Tom Hall, has a greyhound in the first race at Carntyne tonight. Its name is Wee Rose and he reckons it's a certainty to win. Tom's been keepin' its trial times under wraps. This will be the dog's first start at Carntyne and will be a good price, so keep that to yourself. I just thought, with your extra wages, you have a chance to clean up. If you back it each way, you'll bound to at least get your money back if it only runs a place. That's unlikely, though, Jock. Tom reckons Wee Rose will romp home. I'm only tellin' you for what ye did for my brother."

"Well, thanks Eddie ... I'll think about it."

"The first race is at 6 o'clock so you've got time to get down to the betting shop, Jock."

Jock left the pit in a pensive mood. Even with his double wage packet, there still wasn't enough there to clear his debts. If he bet his total wage on Wee

Rose to win at odds of four or five to one, however, he'd be in the clear when she won, as long as he gambled no more.

At five minutes to six, he bet all his money and stood by the door of the betting shop. The odds were five to one and as the race began, he listened to the commentary with trepidation, praying silently for a change in his fortunes.

Wee Rose was pipped at the post, a half-head behind the favourite. With a sinking feeling in his gut, Jock turned and quietly walked out the door.

With not a penny in his pocket, Jock started the long walk home, along the canal bank. He was disappointed but, with his run of bad luck, not surprised. He was leg-weary after the strenuous work involved in freeing Charlie from the suffocating rubble. The further he walked, the more despondent he became. He reflected on the cave-in. All the biggest stones had fallen on his side of the seam. If he hadn't gone for a leak, he would certainly have been killed outright. For the first time ever, he began to think that Jeannie and the bairns would be better off without him. If he kicked the bucket, his wife would be eligible for a widow's pension. The pension wasn't much but, compared to the meagre amount he'd been chipping in, it would be a windfall for Jeannie. At last, he saw the dim lights of Auchinstarry up ahead. That's where he'd leave the canal and turn left across the bridge to Kilsyth. He wasn't looking forward to facing Jeannie. She wouldn't berate him with yelling and screaming. No, much worse ... she'd look at him pityingly and the tears and quiet sobbing would pierce his soul, worse than any physical pain. Thrusting his hands deep into his empty pockets, he trudged wearily in the cold night air along the narrow canal footpath.

Chapter 4

A vigil for a desperate wife,
More turmoil in a troubled life

*W*hen the clock ticked past seven o'clock at night, Jeannie gave up, knowing full well that Jock had let her down again. She'd already fed Jim and Alec on soup and toast and, by the time she given wee Kate her bottle, she went to bed, not caring now whether Jock came home that night or not. She imagined him in an all-night poker school, still searching for that elusive pot of gold. There was no longer any love in the marriage and sex between them was a thing of the past. The truth is that, if Joe had propositioned her that afternoon, she would have willingly gone to bed with him. However, Joe Lennox was such a gentleman, he would never have put her in a position to prostitute herself to feed her bairns. Be that as it may, in a few days, it appears likely that she'd have to beg again and, perhaps this time, she would offer herself to him. With that scenario running through her mind, she fell into a deep sleep.

Jeannie awoke at daybreak, feeling refreshed. Jock had still not returned and she was contemplating reporting him missing but, first things first … she fed Kate and had a cup of tea before rousing the two boys. She fed them tea and toast for breakfast and waved them off to school.

At nine o'clock, there was a loud rap on the front door. Immediately, she thought, "That's a copper's knock."

She opened the door to two policemen. Sergeant Bailey said, "Can we come in, Jeannie?"

"Aye, Sergeant, come away through ... it's aboot Jock, isn't it?"

"Aye, lass, bad news, I'm afraid ... he was fished out the canal this morning at Auchinstarry ... drowned, Jeannie."

"Who found him, Sergeant?"

"Young Constable Martin here, on his way to work. He lives at Auchinstarry, his folks have the farm there."

The constable said, "I was cycling along the canal footpath towards the bridge when I saw the body, face down, snagged on some reeds at the side of the canal. I pulled him on to the bank and turned him over. I checked his pulse and ascertained that he was not breathing."

"Did you recognise him, Constable?" said Jeannie.

"No, Mrs MacDonald. I rode back to the farm to phone the sergeant and asked him to ring the coroner."

"The coroner picked me up," said Sergeant Bailey. "When we arrived at the scene, I recognised Jock straight away."

"Where is Jock now?" asked Jeannie.

"He's in the morgue, Jeannie. Can you come with us and officially confirm the identity?"

"Aye, but I'll have to take the bairn with me."

The coroner pulled back the sheet to reveal the face and looked enquiringly at Jeannie. She nodded and quickly turned away, fighting back the tears.

"Have ye got the clothes he was wearin'?" she asked.

"Yes, Mrs Macdonald," said the coroner, "but they were saturated and clinging to him and I had to cut them off to examine the body properly ... to determine the cause of death, you understand."

"But surely drowning was the cause," said Jeannie, "I dinnae understand at all."

"It was, Mrs MacDonald," said the coroner, "but we couldn't be certain until we examined the body for other injuries."

Jeannie looked mystified and the coroner looked at Sergeant Bailey for support. "It's standard procedure, Jeannie," said the sergeant, "he may have been struck or knifed in the back ... dead before being thrown into the canal."

"Oh, I see," said Jeannie, "but you found nothing, so it was suicide ... right?"

"Well, Jeannie, it was dark, he may have slipped down the slope and couldn't get back up," said the sergeant, "we have no way of knowing, lass."

"Has anybody been through his pockets, Sergeant?"

"Not yet, Jeannie, his clothes were soaking wet. They put them in the next room to dry out. They might be dry enough now if you'd like to check them out."

The sergeant led Jeannie to the adjacent room and pointed to the cut-up pieces of clothing. Jeannie said, "Aye, they're dry enough." She turned the pockets of the moleskin trousers inside out and the sole content was a pay packet with payslip showing the wage details. However, as Jeannie expected, there was no money.

"What are you thinking, Jeannie?"

"Well, Sergeant, when he didn't come home last night, I guessed he was gamblin' at some all-night card game. He's done that before. So, I'm thinkin' he's lost everything and done away wi' himself rather than come home empty-handed. Gamblin' is a terrible weakness, a disease, in fact."

"Aye, there's no doubt about that, lass. Come on, we're done here. Let's get you and the bairn home, Jeannie. I'll make some enquiries and try and trace his movements since leaving the pit. Wi ll you be all right, Jeannie? Is there anything I can do?"

"No, Sergeant, you've been kind. My two boys will be home shortly from school. I've just got to manage on ma own, as usual. It sounds terrible but what I feel now is relief. He was never really with us as a husband or a daddy to the boys. They hardly ever saw him. Now, he's gone and I hope he's at rest. Aye, Jock's troubles are over."

Chapter 5

The rumours will spread thick and fast,
but the gambler's wife is free at last.

$\mathcal{T}$he news of Jock MacDonald's demise spread quickly through the town and, as is the way in these matters, everybody had their own opinion about it.

The following morning, Jeannie was visited by Alan Curle, the manager of Twechar pit. "Mrs MacDonald, I'm sorry for your loss. Your husband was the most reliable worker I've ever had. Tell me, have you made any arrangements for the funeral?"

"No, Mr Curle, I've got no money put away for that. It looks like he'll be buried in a pauper's grave."

"Well, we would like to give him a proper funeral. If you agree, we'll take care of everything. We'll provide the coffin, pay the undertaker, and contact the minister, or priest, on your behalf."

"We're Presbyterian, Mr Curle, but why are ye goin' to all that trouble?"

"The mine owners feel indebted to your husband ... they regard him as a hero for his actions yesterday."

"A hero!" exclaimed Jeannie, incredulously. "I know nothin' aboot this, Mr Curle. Apart from the police, you're the only one to come to this hoose. I don't understand."

"I see. Well, there was a cave-in at the coal face yesterday and Charlie Feeney was buried under the rocks and rubble. Your man, single-handedly, dug him out and saved Charlie's life. He also prevented a lot of bad publicity for the owners if Charlie had died."

"My God, I've never imagined Jock as a hero. I'm afraid he had a gambling problem which didn't do much good for his family, so I'm grateful for your help, Mr Curle."

"So, I can go ahead, Mrs MacDonald?"

"Aye, ye can."

"There's something else ... you'll be able to get a widow's pension but until that comes about, our management has authorized me to give you £10 cash to tide you over."

Jeannie burst into tears. "Thanks, Mr Curle, I'll be able to feed ma bairns properly now."

When Alan Curle had gone, Jeannie sat down, flabbergasted by the turn of events. Who would have imagined Jock MacDonald as a hero? Jeannie knew within herself that the so-called heroic act was not something Jock would ever have laid claim to. She was aware of the coal miners' culture. It was simply mateship, a bond fostered by the necessity to look after each other. Still, it appeared that her man had been true to the code ... if only he'd been as true to his family and brought home his wages. At least, she could now go to Joe Lennox in the morning and repay him.

In the afternoon, she had another unexpected visitor, Mr Pottinger, her landlord.

"Hello, Jeannie, I've heard about your man's death and I don't suppose you really need visitors but I come with some good news for you in your time of sorrow."

"And just what would that be, Mr Pottinger?"

"I'll come straight to the point, Jeannie ... you owe me nothing."

"Aw, Mr Pottinger, how can that be? We're months behind wi' the rent."

"Jeannie, it was Jock who signed the rent agreement, not you. We've written off the debt, so you are in the clear."

"I hear what you're saying, Mr Pottinger but that's really no' fair to you, is it?"

"Oh, perhaps not, Jeannie, but that is the law. Now, you'll be getting a widow's pension ... have you applied for one yet?"

"Oh, no, not yet, I wouldn't know how to do that."

"That's exactly why I brought the forms with me. Have a look, Jeannie ... all you have to do is sign on the bottom and I'll use my influence with the authorities to process it quickly."

"But why are **you** goin' to all this trouble for me, Mr Pottinger?"

"Because I know you as a decent, honest woman, and I would welcome you as a tenant in your own right. I feel so strongly about your unfortunate situation that you can live here rent-free until your pension comes through. With my help, that won't be long."

The boys came home from school. She fed them soup and bread, still courtesy of Joe. Then, she was faced with the problem of telling them about their father. As it happened, they listened and heard that he wouldn't be coming home ever again. To Jeannie's astonishment, they appeared very stoical about the news but, deep in her heart, she realized that her husband had been a virtual stranger to her sons and their reaction was therefore unsurprising.

The boys were outside, kicking a ball around in the street with the neighbouring kids when Sergeant Bailey arrived. "Hello, Jeannie, how are you today?"

"I'm fine, Sergeant ... Mr Curle has been here and the pit owners are goin' to pay for a funeral."

"I know, Jeannie, and it's only right that they should. I've been at the pit and got the whole story. I've managed to trace Jock's movements after he was interviewed by Alan Curle and praised for his action. Curle sent him to the pay clerk who told Jock he'd been given a bonus and his wage this week would be almost doubled. The pay clerk told me that Jock probably went to the betting shop."

"That d0esn't surprise me, Sergeant ... all that money would be burnin' a hole in his pocket. He just couldn't wait to invest it, as he would say. I can guess the rest ... he blew the lot, didn't he?"

"You're right, Jeannie. I spoke to Frank Shepherd at the betting shop. He told me that Jock emptied his pay packet on the counter and bet it all on a dog in the first race. As soon as he heard that he'd lost, he walked straight out. Frank went outside to have a consoling word with Jock but your man was already walking along the canal bank."

"So, Sergeant, I was right ... he did away wi' himself."

"We don't know that, Jeannie. He'd had a hard day ... he must have been tired. He walked because he didn't have even a few pennies for bus fare. There's a steep slope on the footpath at Auchinstarry. My guess is that, in the dark, he slipped down the slope into the canal. He probably tried to climb back out but his heavy pit boots dragged him under. The coroner agrees and will record accidental death."

"Aw Jesus, Sergeant, if only that were true ..."

"Let's give him the benefit of the doubt, lass. It will be better for all concerned, especially your wee boys."

"Thanks, Sergeant ... you've been very kind. I'll be all right now."

Chapter 6

Papa Joe sets the wheels in motion
with the Good Samaritan's continued devotion.

The following day, Jeannie wheeled Kate in the pram to Joe Lennox's shop, just before he closed for lunch. "Hello, Joe, I suppose ye've heard the news?"

"Yes, Jean, word gets around ... how are you feeling?"

"Between you and me, Joe, I feel nothing but relief. I had no love for him ... he killed any feelings I had for him long ago. Officially, it's recorded as accidental death but I know better. He did away wi' himself, Joe, and it's the best thing he's ever done for me and the bairns. He was never goin' to cure the addiction. Does that sound terrible to you, Joe?"

"No, lass, no one knows better than me what you've been going through. I love you, Jean, and I've hated to see you struggling to survive."

As Jeannie heard those words, she rushed into his arms. "I've grown to love you too, Joe, but I couldna do anything aboot it while Jock was alive."

"I want to marry you, lass, but a few months will have to pass. In a wee town like this, tongues would be wagging if they knew about our feelings for each other ... you understand that, don't you, Jean?"

"Only too well, Joe, but ..."

"Listen, Jean, nothing would give me greater pleasure than to take you to bed right now but, I know this town ... the eyes and ears are everywhere. The last thing I want is to besmirch your good name."

"You're a good man, Joe, too good for the likes o' me. You could've had me any time you liked, long ago, for what you've done for me and ma bairns."

"I know that, lass, but I didn't want to take advantage unless I was convinced you felt for me what I felt for you."

"Oh, Joe, what happens now?"

"Can you be patient, Jean, for a wee while?"

"Oh, Joe, I can wait as long as I have to, now that we have an understanding. Actually, I can pay you what I owe you now, Joe. The pit bosses gave me ten pounds and I'll be getting' a widow's pension soon."

"Jean, we are more or less betrothed now ... you owe me nothing, so let's fill your basket now with anything you need. You'll not be going hungry ever again."

"Oh, Joe, you're the best thing that ever happened to me and I long for the day when we can be together."

"Well, my love, it could be sooner than you think. I have some news of my own which has kept me busy. I've been in the process of selling this business. It has been bought by the Co-operative Wholesale Society, the CWS. They have offered me a position on the board, because of my success as a retailer over a long period of time. My job will be commissioning new grocery stores as the Co-op expands operations all over Scotland. That will be an important and ongoing task and I will enjoy that. Now, Jean, I shall be moving to a company house in Bishopbriggs in about a month or so and I shall need a housekeeper. Would you like the job as live-in housekeeper? Naturally, your bairns would come with you."

"Oh, Joe, it sounds too good to be true. We'd be away from the village gossipmongers and could live as man and wife."

"That's exactly what I was thinking, Jean, and we'll have a proper church wedding in six months, when it will all be respectable, even to the gossipmongers. How does that sound, lass?"

"It sounds like paradise, Joe ... and only a month or so away."

"Good ... now as my wife-to-be, here's twenty pounds to make sure you can pay your way ... shop at my old store, now the Co-op, and feed our bairns in the way all bairns should be fed."

"Joe, you are a saint. I only hope that I can live up to your expectations."

Joe lost no time getting established in his new role. He spent the next month commissioning four new sites in the greater Glasgow area before the company house in Bishopbriggs was declared ready for his occupancy.

Chapter 7

Jean's life takes on a brand-new look,
As housekeeper, gardener, and gourmet cook.

"Well, Jean, here we are," said Joe, "what do you think of our house?"

"Oh, Joe, I'm speechless," gasped Jeannie, "this is a mansion. As soon as you turned the car into that tree-lined driveway, I knew you weren't takin' me to a wee council hoose."

"It used to be owned by a doctor, Jean. When he moved away to Aberdeen, the Co-op bought it and here we are. Do you like it?"

"How could I no' like it, Joe, a fully-furnished hoose with a big kitchen, no' jist a wee scullery? It has an inside lavatory and a proper bathroom as well. I love it. I feel like a toff!"

"Good, lass. I've enrolled the boys in the local primary school. It has a fine reputation and a headmaster I liked at first sight."

That night, Jeannie and Joe slept together for the first time. Jeannie was pleasantly surprised by the vigour and passion of her new husband. She responded enthusiastically until they were both spent. "Joe, darling, are you sure you're 40?"

Joe laughed, "So you think I might be 50, do you?"

Jeannie cuddled close to him and said, "Quite the opposite, Joe … you make love like a 26-year-old. I've never had an experience like that in a' ma married life. You are wonderful. I now wonder why they call you Papa Joe."

"Well, Jean, before I got married, I was making a lot of money and became a bit of a soft touch for people collecting for charities. One such woman impressed me and invited me to see the orphanage which she managed. On the following Sunday, I met her and she showed me around. She must've been doing a good job because the kids of all ages seemed happy. I gave her a donation and, as I took my leave, I promised to drop in regularly to check up on any urgent needs. Naturally, as more and more bairns were accepted into the place, the needs were always urgent. I visited every month and gave what I could afford. After a while, I was welcomed spontaneously by the kids. One day, a 4-year-old girl came into my arms and called me Papa Joe. The name stuck and I even named my shop Papa Joe's Store. So, there you are, Jean … it had nothing to do with age, just the affection of a wee orphan lassie."

"That's a lovely story, Joe … you are a good man. Do you still visit the orphanage?"

"No, the manager became ill and died. Without her business acumen and dedication, the place folded and the kids were sent to other orphanages all over the country."

As time passed, Joe went from strength to strength in the Co-op and expanded his role. Now, he was dealing with financiers, lawyers, and investors.

Jeannie gradually got used to having more cash at her disposal than she had ever been used to. She bought cookery books and experimented with dishes quite foreign to her experience. She tried them out on Joe and he always seemed appreciative of her efforts.

One evening, after a roast beef meal, he complimented her and said, "Jean, you seem to enjoy cooking and you do it very well."

"Oh, I do enjoy it, Joe. I never had the money to buy the best joints of meat before. I'm pleased you like what I put on the table."

"Well," said Joe, "I have a couple coming down from Inverness. Our board has appointed the man general manager of Inverness Co-op. I'm the board member designated to entertain them before they go back home. You could be a big help to me if you put on a meal for them, a wee dinner party, on Friday night ... just Angus and Kirsty Stewart, you and me. Do you think you can handle that?"

"Och, I can cook a nice roast if ye like but you're forgetting that I'm your hoosekeeper, no' your wife. I won't be sittin' doon at the table."

"You know, Jean, I never thought of that," mused Joe, thoughtfully stroking his chin. "Yes, it's probably better if you play the housekeeper until I can make an honest woman of you."

Friday evening arrived and Joe welcomed his guests. When Jeannie came from the kitchen with roast lamb, potatoes, parsnip, swede turnip, and garden peas, he introduced her. "This is Jean, my housekeeper and cook."

When they finished the first course, Jeannie cleared away the plates and returned with a raspberry trifle. Kirsty complimented her on the roast and said she was sure she was going to enjoy the trifle.

Jeannie thanked her and added, "The raspberries are frae the garden, freshly picked this afternoon."

After the meal, Kirsty insisted on helping with the washing-up, but Jeannie said, "Och, there's nae need for that. I'm sure ye hae business to discuss wi' Joe. Thanks jist the same but I'll be fine."

"Joe and Angus have details to talk over," said Kirsty, "I'm not involved, so let me help you. Besides, I want to pick your brains about your cooking. I have to tell you that was the best meal I've had in years."

So, overwhelmed by the success of her first dinner party, Jeannie led Kirsty to the kitchen and handed her an apron. "We cannae have your beautiful dress gettin' dirty."

As Jeannie washed and Kirsty dried, Kirsty said, "Now tell me your secret, how do you manage to make your food so tasty?"

"Och, Kirsty, there's nae secret aboot it ... I jist follow the recipe books, word for word."

"Oh, come on, you are far too modest. Look, I'm a doctor, a GP, and we have a cook who does the evening meals for us on weekdays. I dabble in the kitchen on weekends only but we only have easy-to-make snacks then. Now, our cook works from recipes too but her stuff would not hold a candle to yours. There's more to it than what you are telling me. Now, I understand that chefs do not like to reveal their techniques but, as you and I will probably never meet again, I thought you might break the rules."

"I don't know whit more I can say, Kirsty. To tell ye the God's honest truth, I didn't take cookin' seriously until Joe offered me the hoosekeeper job. I have two wee boys and a wee lassie ... I think I got the job because Joe felt sorry for me, a poor, strugglin' widow."

"I see ... well, Jean, you have a gift. Joe is lucky to have you. Now, it's none of my business but, as a woman, I couldn't help noticing the look in Joe's eyes as he introduced you. You're a bit more than his housekeeper, aren't you?"

"Oh dear, here we are, Joe and me, thinkin' we were that clever, but along you came, our first visitor, and saw through us straightaway. Oh, well, what's done is done."

"There's no cause for concern, Jean, I won't be telling anybody, not even Angus. He's a mere male ... he wouldn't have noticed anything. As I said, Jean, it's none of my business."

"Well, I want to tell you the whole story anyway, Kirsty. It'll no' take long. Ma man died three months ago. He'd been a gambler and didnae provide properly for his family. If it hadn't been for the generosity of Joe Lennox, we'd have gone hungry. Naturally, I was grateful to Joe and I knew he'd always had a soft spot for me. He always behaved like a perfect gentleman, though. When he asked me to be his hoosekeeper, I jumped at the chance and we've been real close ever since. We'll be married in another three months, a decent time after ma man's death. In a wee toon, ye have to be mindful of these things. Well, that's it, Kirsty."

"I'm happy for you both, Jean. I suppose it will be a quiet wedding?"

Jeannie laughed, "Aye, it will, Kirsty, but I'd love you to be matron of honour. Is that asking too much of you? ... I mean I've only just met ye but I like ye. You're as straight as a die."

"I'd be honoured, Jean ... I'm sure we're going to be good friends."

After Joe waved to Angus and Kirsty as they left, he went inside. "Well, my bonny Jean, I was very proud of you tonight. You put on a magnificent spread and you certainly impressed Kirsty. Did you get on well with her in the kitchen, lass?"

"Oh, I did, Joe, although I was fair intimidated by the two of them earlier."

"Really? That surprises me ... I thought they were very friendly right from the start."

"Oh, they were, Joe. That wasn't ma problem. It was the way they spoke ... almost like those English newsreaders on the wireless. I was ashamed to open ma mooth in front o' them. I mean, I've had nae education to speak of ... as I said, I felt intimidated. Are they English?"

"No, lass, they come from Inverness. People from Inverness are reputed to speak the English language better than anyone else in the British Isles. However, be that as it may, Jean, you shouldn't let that bother you. There's nothing wrong with the way you speak. Most folk in the Glasgow area talk just like you. That's the way it is in a working-class environment. I'm sure Kirsty wasn't fazed by it."

"Oh, no, Joe, once we got talkin', I relaxed and we had a good auld natter. She's lovely, Joe. By the way, she knows that you and I are together, soon to be married."

"Really, Jean? I'm surprised you let that cat out of the bag."

"Ye've got that wrong, Joe, it was you. She saw the look in your eyes when you introduced me and, smart woman that she is, jaloused that I wasn't jist your hoosekeeper. She's agreed to be ma matron of honour when we get spliced."

"My God, you two must have got on like a house on fire. That's great, Jean. I think I'll ask Angus to be best man. I've got an even better suggestion ... why don't we take the bairns on a wee holiday and get married in Inverness. Would you like that, lass?"

"Oh, Joe, that sounds lovely ... I've never been further than Glasgow. There's jist one thing I'd like to do in the next three months."

"And what would that be, my bonny Jean?"

"I'd like to be able to talk properly, Joe ... no' like the Inverness folk but jist like you. You talk Scottish but ye do it properly. Could ye teach me to sound like you?"

"Oh, lassie, I'm not a teacher but, if you're really determined, I'll hire a personal tutor for you."

"Thanks, Joe, and there's one more thing ... I liked it when you introduced me as Jean. After all, that's what I was christened."

"Oh, my bonny lass, I've always preferred Jean to Jeannie, anyway ... that was my mother's name. Yes, she was Jean."

Two days later, as Jean was clearing away the breakfast dishes, there was a knock at the front door. She opened the door to find a young man with a brief case. "Good morning, my name is Jeremy Cowan. Joe Lennox asked me to come and see you ... you must be Jean, right?"

"Aye, that's right ... how can I help ye?"

"Joe said you needed some help with your speech. I'm not really sure what he meant, Jean. He said you'd explain."

"Oh, my God, I don't know how to start. I suppose I'd jist like to be able to speak like you. Anyway, come in ... I was jist aboot to put the kettle on ... would ye like a cuppa tea?"

"That would be lovely, Jean."

As Jean went into the kitchen, Jeremy noticed some recipe books on the coffee table. He picked one up and leafed through it and, when Jean returned and handed him the tea, he said, "There's a recipe here for whiting supreme, Jean. Could you read it out to me?"

Jean's face lit up, pleasantly surprised at the request. She read the recipe and, when she finished, she asked if that was a favourite meal of his.

"I've never had it, Jean ... to be honest, I just wanted to test your reading skills."

"Och, I've got nae trouble readin', Jeremy."

"Yes, you read it beautifully ... in perfect English too. That makes my job a lot easier, Jean."

"I don't understand, Jeremy, I'm sorry."

"OK, I'm going to write something down and I want you to read it back to me."

He handed her the sheet of paper and she read, "I don't understand, Jeremy. I have no trouble reading. I'd just like to be able to speak like you."

"There you are, Jean ... you have just spoken like me."

"Aye, but they were your words, no' mine, Jeremy. It's easy for you. You've always spoke properly, I daresay ... wi' a posh name like Jeremy, no doubt you were brought up in a hoose where yer family were well educated."

"Jean, you couldn't be more wrong. I was born and raised in a Gorbals slum where everybody spoke the local street language. I was the youngest of three children and was lucky enough to win a scholarship to the university. I had to learn to speak properly, as you call it, just to be understood by the lecturers, who weren't all Scottish."

"I see," said Jean, "and how did ye learn, Jeremy?"

"By reading and practising what I read until it became second nature. If you're prepared to put in the effort, I guarantee you'll achieve your ambition in no time."

"I'm ready, Jeremy, jist tell me whit tae do."

"Well, we'll just have a wee chat, like two old pals, for the next hour or so. I'll be making notes as we go along. When we're finished, I'll be leaving you with homework to do, OK?"

"Whatever you say, lad, you're the teacher."

At the end of the hour, Jeremy handed her his notes, consisting of her responses which he had written in proper English. "Practise reading those out loud during the day. When Joe comes home, he may be surprised by your progress. I'll see you in two days, same time, OK?"

"Fine, Jeremy, I jist hope I'm no' wastin' yer time."

"Joe asked me if I'd be available to help you over the next three months. Trust me, Jean, you'll be fine, long before that."

One month later, Jeremy advised Joe that Jean didn't need his services any longer.

"She's made remarkable progress, Jeremy, thanks to you," said Joe.

"Joe, to be frank, I merely set her on the right path," said Jeremy. "She is intelligent, highly literate, for someone who left school at 13 years of age."

"Well, Jeremy, whatever the reason, Jean now has a lot of self-confidence and she would not have gained that without you. You're still at uni, aren't you?"

"Yes, Joe, I'm halfway through."

"How are you fixed for money? Right now, I feel as if I haven't paid you enough."

"Joe, you've been more than generous ... the scholarship will see me through."

"OK, then, Jeremy ... I'll keep in touch. I'd like to know what career path you take when you get your degree. By the way, Jean has been curious as to how you came to be called Jeremy, bearing in mind your Gorbals background."

Jeremy laughed, "I don't like to talk about it but I've grown fond of Jean so I'll tell you. When I won that scholarship, my mother told me how the name came about. She said that when I was a baby, she looked into my eyes and saw something special. She just knew that I was going to amount to something, so she gave me a classy name to help me on my way."

"Well, laddie, your mother was right. I'll tell Jean ... she'll be delighted. Good luck, Jeremy."

Jean hosted another dinner party comprising the board of C.W.S and their wives. According to Joe, she acquitted herself brilliantly and he proudly introduced her as his wife-to-be. Jean accepted the congratulations along with the many accolades regarding her cooking. She spoke confidently, having lost all her previous nervousness. She privately drank a toast to her mentor, Jeremy Cowan, with whom she determined to keep in touch.

The school summer holidays arrived and Joe, with the help of Angus Stewart, organised the wedding arrangements. "Well, Jean, my love, are you ready to take the plunge?"

"Ready and willing, Joe, and the two boys are looking forward to a highland holiday. The wee girl is still too young to appreciate it but we can't leave her behind, can we?"

Joe and Jean laughed at such an outrageous idea.

The family enjoyed the magnificent scenery en route before booking into the Royal Highland Hotel, Inverness, in time for a sumptuous evening meal.

Jean was most impressed, not only by the food but also by the ambience of the classic hotel.

"Joe, that was a great dinner."

"Yes, my love, almost as good as the meals you serve up."

"Oh, now I know you're joking."

"On the contrary, Jean, in the short time you've been experimenting with recipes previously beyond your reach, you've come on by leaps and bounds. With your enthusiasm, you'll add to your repertoire and will match this hotel's kitchen, and any other, I daresay. I'm really proud of you but now I have to keep an eye on my weight, so tasty and irresistible are the meals coming out of **your** kitchen."

Kirsty and Angus called in after breakfast, to take the family to the Registrar, where a simple marriage ceremony took place.

Angus then took them to his house where they partook of a light lunch. Kirsty had a long chat with Jean in the kitchen, noticing almost immediately that Jean was now speaking the King's English, albeit with a Scottish accent. Kirsty politely refrained from comment but Jean told her the whole story, singing the praises of her mentor, the young student, Jeremy Cowan. "He'll be my friend for life, Kirsty. I'll be following his career with interest."

"I hope you'll be staying a few days in Inverness, Jean."

"No, Kirsty, we're not going to interrupt your busy schedule. You and Angus have done your duty by us as Matron of Honour and best man. After lunch, we want to head across country to Aberdeen and travel down the east coast to our capital, Edinburgh. Our honeymoon is going to be a learning experience for me and my family."

"Jean, I reckon you are going to be Joe's biggest asset. He's lucky to have you as his wife. Now, don't be strangers ... you'll always be welcome here."

When they arrived home, Jean and Joe settled quickly into their now completely legal marriage, blissfully happy in a union based on love and mutual respect.

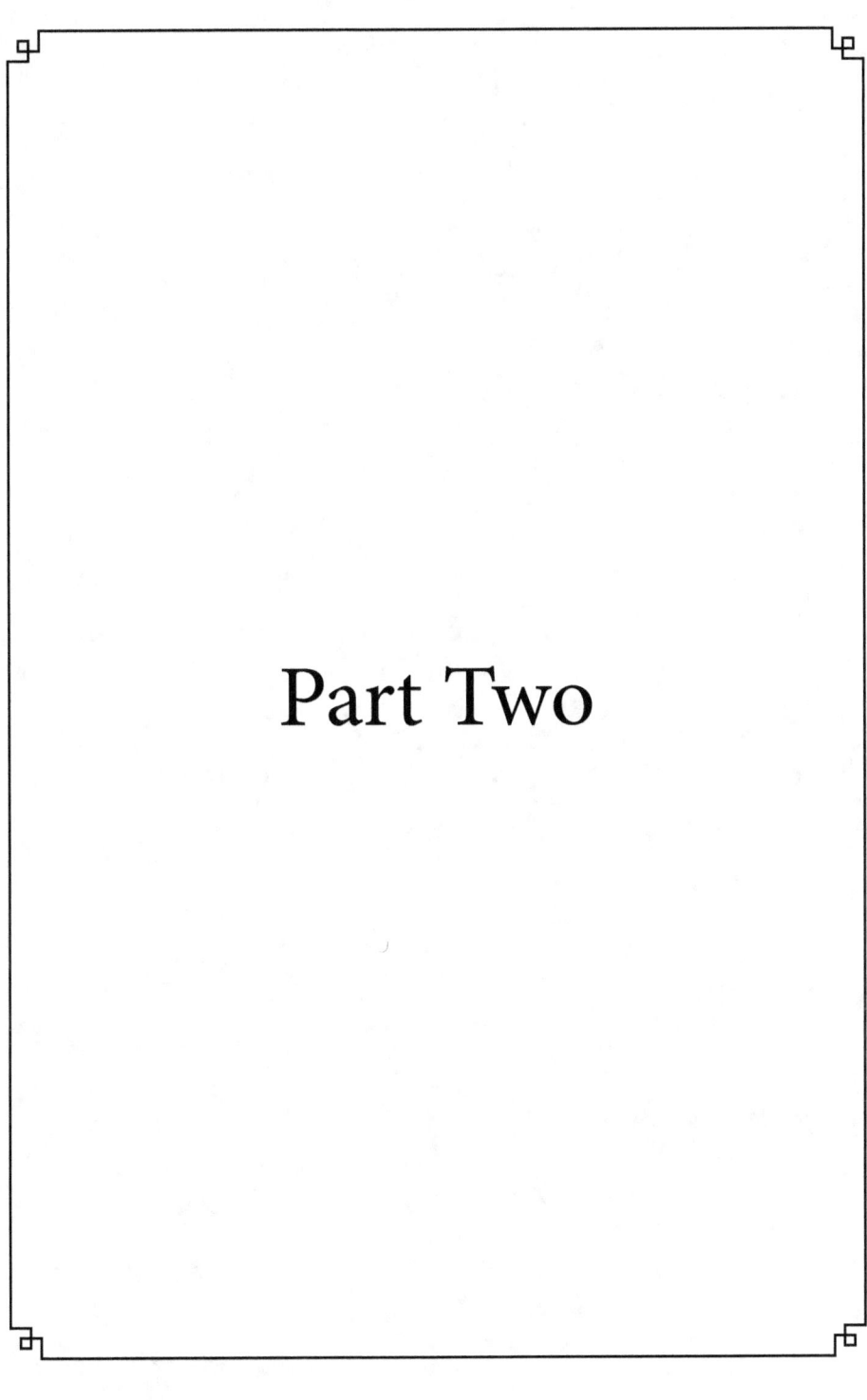

Part Two

Chapter 8

Joe and Jean could be forgiven
for claiming their marriage made in heaven

*I*t was now 1935. Four years had slipped past without a disagreement.

"How lucky am I to have a man who loves my bairns and takes an interest in all their activities?" mused Jean. "I've never had a reason to criticise anything he does."

As time went by, Joe realised that he was not destined to father any children of his own. This gave him no cause for concern as he had grown fond of Jean's bairns, although he'd never had the urge to adopt them. He had discussed the matter with Jean and she had no firm views about it. He was perfectly happy for the bairns to address him as Joe. Alec was now 12 and had successfully completed his primary school education. A choice had to be made about where to place him for his secondary education. The boy seemed keen on technical subjects, and he was always reading magazines on aeronautics.

"What would you like to do when you finish your schooling, Alec?" asked Joe.

"Oh, I don't really know, Joe," said Alec, "I like aeroplanes but can you get a proper job in that line or do you have to join the air force? I don't know enough about it."

"Well, would you like to be a pilot or build the planes, son?"

"Is it possible to do both, Joe?"

"Yes, Alec, I should think so. The way to go is to study hard at your maths and science at school and then do an engineering course at college. I'm sure you could specialise in aeronautical engineering later. Does that sound good to you?"

"It sounds great, Joe, but what about the flying?"

"Well, when you're a bit older, you could join the Glasgow Flying Club and learn to fly. I see in one of your magazines an article about Tiger Moths. I know that the flying club have a couple of those."

"Crikey, Joe, that would be terrific ... flying a Tiger Moth would be a dream come true."

On the strength of young Alec's qualifying exam marks, Joe had no trouble getting him accepted as a pupil at Allan Glen's School. This was a famous institution which produced many people who excelled in science and engineering. Alec was over the moon and soon settled in. He was introduced to the game of rugby, once described as a ruffian's game played by gentlemen. Alec was extrovert by nature, physically courageous, and fleet of foot. He took to the game with enthusiasm and soon made the 1st fifteen, as a full back. Joe reckoned he had chosen wisely. "Enjoy your sport, Alec, but never forget your main aim ... remember the Tiger Moths."

Jean was a trifle worried. "That sounds like a pretty flash school, Joe. Can we afford to have him there?"

"Yes, Jean, we can ... I think it will prove to be a good investment. He's made of the right stuff, our Alec. He deserves to be given every opportunity. Young Jim still has another year to go at primary school. When it's his turn, I'll have a talk to him and find out what **he** wants to do in later life."

"Joe, you would have to be the best stepfather that ever lived. I love you."

A few evenings later, Jeremy Cowan dropped in to see them. "How's married life?" he said, "as if I didn't know. If there was ever a marriage made in heaven, this is it."

"We're happy, Jeremy. I've been thinking of you ... wondering how you're getting on," said Jean.

"I'm still at uni, doing a post-graduate course in law."

"So, you got your degree then, Jeremy?" asked Joe.

"Yes, Joe, Bachelor of Law. I can put LLB after my name. Hopefully, by the end of this term, I'll be Master of Law, LLM."

"Are you still funded by the scholarship?"

"Yes, fortunately, Joe. My results in the degree course prompted the powers-that-be to extend the scholarship. I'm sorry I haven't been in touch ... been flat out studying."

"I understand, Jeremy," said Joe. "Can you promise me one thing?"

"Of course, Joe, you only have to name it."

"When you get your LLM, come and see me before you decide what's next on your agenda."

"I promise, Joe, and now, I have to run. I'll see you both at end of term, win or lose."

Joe was on the crest of a wave, recognised by his fellow board members as a person of great ability as well as being a gentleman of integrity. Therefore, it came as no surprise that, when the Chairman of the board resigned for health reasons, Joe was unanimously elected to the top job. From then on, although Joe, as CEO, was busier than ever in the office, he was able to be home every night with the family. He now could delegate the away from home tasks as and when required.

He relaxed at home playing the piano and encouraged the family to sing along. He was pleasantly surprised to discover that Jean possessed a good soprano voice and sang in tune, never deviating from the key. He adhered to the popular songs of the day, simple melodies which posed no difficulties for the boys. Although enthusiastic, they each could be classed as having a fair voice but a rough passage.

Joe always went to work on Saturday mornings when he usually had the office to himself and could ascertain that there were no loose ends which has escaped his notice.

One Saturday, as he entered the house at midday, he heard the piano tinkling in the living room. To his surprise, he found young Kate, standing at the keyboard, playing 'You are my sunshine' with one finger only but in perfect rhythm, humming the melody as she played. He did not interrupt her but crept away to the kitchen where Jean was preparing lunch. "Jean, Jean, wee Kate's playing a real tune on the piano."

"Oh, she's been doing that for a while. She can play three tunes now. She spends a lot of time in there, Joe ... seems real keen. She's not doing any harm, is she?"

"Not at all, Jean ... I'm just surprised, I mean she's only five years old."

"Could you teach her properly, Joe?"

"No, no, love, I'm not qualified to teach anybody. I just play by ear ... I'm not crash hot on reading music. I could get a real music teacher but I think Kate's a bit too young. Let's just leave it for a while. If she gets fed up with it, well, no harm done."

The weeks passed uneventfully until Jeremy arrived, grinning happily. "Good evening, you lovely people, you may now address me as Jeremy Cowan LLM."

"Well done, Jeremy," said Joe, jumping from his chair to shake his hand.

"Does that mean you're finished with the university, Jeremy?" said Jean.

"Yes, Jean, I'll have to work for a living now."

"Have you decided what you want to do now, Jeremy?" asked Joe.

"Well, I've had a couple of job offers from the largest corporate law firms in Glasgow, Joe."

"They'd pay a pretty good salary for a Master of Law, wouldn't they?"

"Yes, but the work's not what I really want to do, Joe. At this stage, it's only a pipe dream but I have a vision of putting something back into the community where I was raised."

"Go on, Jeremy," said Joe. "Tell me what you have in mind."

"Oh, someday, if I save enough money, I'd like to have a wee office in the Gorbals. There are always folk there in need of legal assistance but can't afford it. I'd like to help if I could, pro bono, where necessary." Jeremy sighed, "As I said, Joe, it's a pipe dream but, as they say, hope springs eternal."

"I see," said Joe, "Do you mind if I change the subject, Jeremy?"

"No, of course not, Joe, what do you want to talk about?"

"Do you know about the job I'm doing now, Jeremy? Are you aware of what the Co-op stands for?"

"Not really, Joe. I've heard you run the show though … some kind of chain of shops, isn't it?"

"Yes, a big chain, getting bigger all the time. Economies of scale means we can buy from our suppliers at a better rate. This will be good news for our customers as we can pass on the savings to them. We don't pass **all** the savings on at the point of sale, however, as that would create commercial upheaval for the smaller retailers in the community. We still retain a reasonable profit margin to pay for our overheads but our opposition have been denied the opportunity to grossly overcharge. At the end of year our customers, who really are our members, receive a cash bonus."

"How do you keep track of all that, Joe?"

"By a simple system. If you went to your local Co-op office to join, you'd be given a membership number along with a book recording your dealings with us. We have our own currency, our own coins made of bakelite. Let's say you bought £5 worth of Co-op tokens every week. At the end of a year, your book would show you'd bought around £250 worth of tokens. If the local dividend was set at, say, 5 shillings in the pound, you'd receive a cash bonus of around £60."

"A nice sum to receive for Christmas," said Jeremy. "I like that idea … every member sharing in the profits."

"Good, now we can get back to your future, Jeremy. I've got a proposition for you. If you reject it, there will be no hard feelings … we'll still be friends."

Jeremy laughed, "My God, this must be serious stuff, Joe. OK, you'd better hit me with it."

"The Co-op is right now organising the lease of a group of retail stores at Gorbals Cross. I can offer you an office there and equip it for you with all the gear you lawyers need. In return, I want you to handle all our legal business. That will be a job well below your capabilities, mainly conveyancing, drawing up contracts, the occasional court case to settle lease disputes, and the like. For that, we'll pay you a retainer, enough for you to live on.

I reckon you'll have plenty of time to build up your own clientele in the community. Now, have a think about it ... it will be a few weeks before the Gorbals deal is finalised."

"Phew," gasped Jeremy, "I'm flabbergasted, Joe. I don't need time to think about it ... it sounds like the best of both worlds. I accept, with gratitude."

"Great, Jeremy, I'm delighted to have you on board. You can start right away. Make a list of the equipment you'll need ... bring it to me at my office on Monday and we'll get started on it. In a few weeks you'll be able to hang out your shingle at Gorbals Cross. It's no longer a pipe dream."

"You've been very kind to me, Joe, and I appreciate it."

"Nonsense, the Co-op is getting the best of the bargain ... a Master of Law."

Joe continued his regular sing-song sessions with the family and was delighted to hear from Jean that wee Kate had not lost interest in the piano. In fact, she had expanded her repertoire of one-finger tunes. "She'll be 6 next week, Joe," said Jean. "Is it time to start her on lessons?"

"It might well be, Jean ... I'll make some enquiries locally about a tutor."

"Actually, I've found a young woman who is a school teacher at the local primary Catholic school," said Jean. "She seems to be well qualified also as a piano tutor. She can come here tomorrow after school to meet Kate. I hope you don't mind, Joe?"

"Mind? Why should I mind, love? Well done ... that saves me the trouble."

"Grace Devine is a Catholic, Joe. I don't know how you stand with that."

"Oh, Jean, Jean, I'm sure Miss Devine is just trying to supplement her income, not trying to convert wee Kate. I'll be a bit later home tomorrow ... Alec has rugby practise tomorrow at Allan Glen's, so you can welcome Miss Devine. I expect she'll be gone by the time we get home."

Next day, Grace Devine arrived at Jean's house before Kate came home from school. "Hello, Jean, am I too early?"

"No, Grace, Kate's not here yet but I wanted a word with you first anyway. When Kate arrives, I'll introduce you as Miss Devine."

"I don't mind if the wee girl calls me Grace."

"Well, I'll tell you why, Grace. She doing really well at school because she respects her teacher, Miss Frew, who is firm but fair with her class. Kate responds to discipline, so I think it wise to place you in the Miss Frew category."

Grace smiled, "That's fine, Jean ... you know your daughter best."

"Once I've introduced you, I'll leave you with her ... I expect you'd prefer that, right?"

"Yes, Jean, I just want to have a wee talk to her before we get to the piano bit. By the way, that is a beautiful instrument. Is there someone in your family who plays?"

"Yes, Joe, my husband, but he doesn't read music too well. He's the one who suggested proper lessons for Kate."

When Kate arrived, Jean said, "This is Miss Devine, a music teacher. She's going to have a talk with you while I start cooking dinner."

"Hello, Miss Devine," said Kate. "Do you want to hear me play?"

"Yes, Kate ... show me what you can do."

Kate played her favourite, 'You are my sunshine', with great confidence, and waited for Miss Devine to speak.

"That was very good, Kate. I'd like you to play it again but this time I'll sit beside you and play the left-hand part."

When they finished, Kate said, "Gee, that was great ... I want to be able to do that, play with both hands."

"You will, Kate. At the moment, you're only using one finger. Shall I show you what it sounds and looks like when I play with both hands?"

"Oh yes, please, Miss."

When Miss Devine played the simple piece, young Kate clapped her hands and said, "Daddy plays with both hands but he's not as good as you, Miss. Can you teach me to play like that?"

"I can, Kate, but first, you have to learn how to read music and practise the proper hand exercises. It will mean a lot of hard work before you play tunes again. How keen are you to learn, Kate? Will you practice one hour every day to start with?"

"Oh yes, Miss Devine ... just show me what to do."

"I'll have a talk with your mum and sort out the best day to get you started."

Jean walked outside with Grace. "Well, Grace, what do you think about our wee Kate?"

"She's as bright as a button, Jean. She has an enquiring mind and she seems really keen on learning the piano. I'm happy to take her as a pupil. At her age, we'll hasten slowly ... give her plenty of time to settle in to a practice routine. I can fit her in on Saturday mornings at 10 o'clock ... is that suitable?"

"That'll be perfect, Grace, so we'll see you tomorrow for her first lesson."

Joe arrived home with Alec and Kate ran to meet him, excitedly, "I'm starting piano lessons with Miss Devine tomorrow. She's lovely ... we played 'You are my Sunshine' together".

"That's great, Kate ... I hear she's a very good teacher."

Jean said, "They got on famously together, Joe ... I think I've chosen well."

"I'm sure you have, Jean ... listen, I wanted to have a chat with young Jim before tea. Is he in his room?"

"Yes, he's up there reading ... he's always got his nose in a book these days."

"Hello, Jim, what's that you're reading?" said Joe.

"It's a history of the Vikings when they came to Scotland, Joe. Do you know much about them?"

"Not really, Jim, but I believe they were a wild bunch. Can I interrupt your reading for a few minutes?"

"Sure, Joe."

"Well, you'll be finishing up at primary school shortly and I thought we could have a wee chat about your future. Have you any idea what you'd like to work at when you finish your education?"

"Not really ... I'm different from Alec. He's always wanted to get into engineering and he's mad about aeroplanes."

"So, you're not mad about any subject, Jim?"

"Well, I like reading about all kinds of stuff ... history, famous people, and all that, but nobody's going to pay me for reading, are they, Joe?"

"Oh well, Jim, you'll have years to find some career that suits you. In the meantime, I'll get you into Allan Glen's school. You'll receive a first-class general education there and they have a great library of books on any subject. Are you happy with that?"

"I will be as long as they don't make me play rugby, Joe."

Joe laughed, "There's no fear of that, Jim ... you can choose your own sport, like running. You like to run, don't you?"

"Yes, I'm pretty fast on my feet ... I'm just no good at team sports."

"Well, Jim, that's settled then. To each his own."

Chapter 9

*The extended family now appears
to become the dynasty of the golden years.*

The next few years were always referred to by Jean as the golden years. Thanks to a generous, loving husband, her two boys were both doing well at one of the most prestigious schools in the land. The wee girl was turning out to be a prodigy, according to Grace Devine. Not only was Kate excelling in all aspects of piano study but she became more enthusiastic as time went by. She begged her mother to let her have two lessons per week because she had perfected Saturday's exercises by Monday. So, Grace came to the house every Wednesday, after school.

On one of those occasions, Jean asked Grace if she like to stay and have dinner. "Joe is bringing home a workmate and friend of the family. I'd like you to meet him, Grace. You may have something in common ... he's done a bit of teaching in his time **and** he's also very handsome."

"I'm not exactly looking for a man, Jean," said an amused Grace.

"Perhaps not, Grace, but you like to have dinner occasionally, don't you?"

"All right, Jean, you win ... I'd love to stay for dinner. May I play your beautiful baby grand piano in the meantime ... sing for my supper, as it were?"

"Oh yes, I'd love that ... I'll be able to hear you from the kitchen, Grace."

Kate sat close to the piano as Grace began to play 'Melody in F', by Rubenstein. Within seconds, the wee girl closed her eyes and listened, enraptured by the music and her tutor's soft touch on the keyboard.

The front door opened and Joe and Jeremy Cowan entered. When they heard the music, they quietly came into the lounge and stood silently at the door. When the music came to an end, both men applauded enthusiastically, whereupon Grace turned to acknowledge the applause. Her gaze fixed on Jeremy and she said, "Where have I seen you before?"

Jeremy smiled, saying, "You've seen me many times, Grace, when you were a teenager. I'm Jeremy Cowan, an old neighbour in Gorbals."

Grace laughed delightedly, "Of course, how could I have forgotten that? You were the clever clogs in our tenement. Everyone said so and they were right ... you went to university, right?"

"Yes, when I was 17, I got a scholarship and lodged with a maiden aunt, in Gilmorehill, from where I could walk to the uni. You were only 11 then, so I'm not surprised you didn't recognise me straight away. You've grown into a beautiful young lady, I must say. I recognised your auburn hair and those smiling Irish eyes."

"Well, my mother was born in Ireland so I've got her genes, I suppose."

"Are you still living at the old address, Grace?"

"No, I live here, in Bishopbriggs, Jeremy. I teach at the local Catholic school and share a flat owned by the school."

Jean came into the lounge and announced that the meal was ready and they adjourned to the dining room where Joe told Jean that Grace and Jeremy knew each other. "Yes, Jean," said Grace, "we grew up together, next door neighbours ... a small world, isn't it?"

"Well, that's lovely," said Jean, "you'll have a lot of catching up to do. I hope you like roast chicken, Grace."

"I do, Jean ... it smells divine, no pun intended."

"Good, let's eat it while it's hot ... then you two can have a nice talk together."

There was limited small talk as the group enjoyed Jean's delightful meal. After dinner, Grace offered to help Jean wash the dishes but Jean said, "No, lass, Joe always dries up for me ... sit down and talk to Jeremy. I told you he was handsome, didn't I?"

"Yes, Jean", said Grace, "but I'd really like to get going now. I have a bit of preparation to do for school tomorrow."

Jeremy heard the last part of their conversation and said, "Let me run you home, Grace ... we can have a wee talk on the way."

As they bid goodnight to the family, Jean caught Grace's eye and winked, smiling, as she escorted them to the door.

"I didn't know you could play the piano, Grace," said Jeremy.

"Well, when you lived next door, we didn't have a piano but shortly after you left, my dad and three of his workmates brought home an old upright piano. You may remember, he was a dustman with the council. My mum asked him how he'd got the money to buy it because he never had a brass razoo, being an alcoholic. He muttered that some guy had asked them to get rid of it for him. It seems it had been his wife's piano and she'd run off with another man. Personally, Jeremy, I now think it 'fell off the back of a truck'. My mum had been taught piano in Ireland and had also done a bit of tutoring there. Anyway, she could see I was interested and started teaching me. I became good enough to win a scholarship to the Scottish Academy of Music and got a Diploma of Music, when I was 18. I've been teaching at Bishopbriggs ever since. I also do a wee bit of tutoring outside school hours. Actually, that's my connection with Joe and Jean ... I've been teaching young Kate since she was 6. She's now 9 and shows great promise."

"That's wonderful, Grace ... and are your parents still in Gorbals?"

"No, Dad died of liver cancer and a year later, Mum remarried, to an Irishman. They now live in Dublin. She writes to me about once a year. Now, tell me what you've been up to, Jem."

Jeremy laughed, "Jem? I haven't been called that since I left Gorbals."

"You don't mind, do you?"

"No, Grace, I think I prefer it. Jeremy is a bit of a mouthful."

"Well, come on then, what's your story, Jem?"

"OK, short and sweet ... scholarship to university, got a master's degree in law; Joe Lennox gave me a job with CWS, along with permission to build up my own business in Gorbals ... everything going well on my front. The bad news is that my parents were killed in an accident last year."

"Oh, I'm sorry, Jem, how did that happen?"

"They were running across the road to catch a bus and were hit by a lorry. The lorry driver didn't have any chance to avoid them."

"Oh, Jesus, what bad luck ... are your sisters still living in Gorbals, Jem?"

"No, they got married and moved away years ago. I get a postcard every year."

"And would ye be havin' a wife now, Jem?"

Jeremy laughed, "Why the Irish accent all of a sudden?"

"Oh, I'm just mimicking my mother ... that's the kind of question she'd have asked you. Well ... **are** you married, Jem?"

"No, not yet, Grace."

"Mm, that sounds like you have someone in mind ... do you?"

"No, not yet, Grace."

"Well, it appears we are a pair of loners."

"In that case, Grace, how'd you like to come for a drive to Loch Lomond on Sunday?"

"That sounds delightful, Jem. I'll go to early mass ... you can pick me up at the church around nine o'clock, if that's convenient. Of course, you can come to mass with me if you like."

"No, I'll give that a miss ... I haven't been to mass since I went to university. I'm a bit of a backslider, you might say. Does that bother you, Grace?"

"Not in the slightest ... the school expects me to be a practising Catholic. That's the only reason I go ... to keep my job. So, I'm a hypocrite ... does that bother you, Jem?"

"Not at all, I'd hate you to be perfect."

As the summer passed, Jeremy and Grace were seeing each other regularly and it appeared that their relationship was getting to the serious stage. Jeremy confided to Joe that he intended to propose marriage to Grace.

"She's a fine lass, Jeremy, and you seem to be well suited ... do you have a particular reason for telling me?" said Joe. "Surely you're not asking for **my** blessing? You look a wee bit concerned ... what's on your mind?"

"You're very perceptive, Joe. I'm sure Grace has been expecting me to propose for a while but I'm worried about the political situation. This fellow, Hitler, is on a mission and I'm pretty sure that Britain will get dragged into a war before long. What's your take on the situation, Joe?"

"I share your opinion. Jeremy, and I understand your problem. If war breaks out, you'll be called up and you don't think it's fair on Grace to marry under the circumstances."

"Exactly, Joe ... what should I do?"

"Tell her what's on your mind and hear what she wants to do. My guess is that she'll understand and agree to wait. She's not a silly young romance-struck lassie ... she's a level-headed woman."

Chapter 10

As World War Two gets under way,
Certain family problems come into play.

On September 3rd, 1939, Britain declared war on Germany and conscription for the armed forces began.

By mutual agreement, Jeremy and Grace deferred not only wedding plans but also any official engagement while the war continued. Jeremy enlisted in the army and was posted to London for basic training. Grace, as a teacher, was in a reserved occupation as all the eligible male teachers had been called up. In addition to her music, she took on extra duties as a primary school teacher after a short training course.

After basic training, Jeremy, because of his outstanding academic qualifications, was sent on an officer training course. He performed excellently, showing leadership potential, was allocated the rank of Captain in the Royal Signals, and ordered to report to Colonel Nicholson at the Ministry of Defence H/Q in London.

"Captain Cowan, at ease, have a seat. I'm Colonel Nicholson ... I've asked you to come here rather than posting you straightaway to a Signals battalion. The reason is I don't really know what to do with you. I've been looking through your record. You volunteered, didn't wait to be called up ... right?"

"Yes Sir, that's correct."

"Why?"

"A sense of duty, Sir ... I'd been following the career of Adolf Hitler for years and knew that, sooner or later, Britain would have to confront him. I felt that quite strongly, Sir."

"Mm, Jeremy, isn't it?"

"Yes Sir."

"Well, Jeremy, most volunteers have a particular goal ... they want to be a pilot, or they want to join the navy because it's been a family tradition. You expressed no definite aim ... that's unusual."

"I fully expected the army to use me in any capacity I could best serve, Sir."

"You have first-class university degrees ... you were top of the group in basic training, showing outstanding fitness for a corporate lawyer. During officer training, you revealed rare leadership qualities. Summing up, Jeremy, you seem to be the complete package. Now, I've been asked to form a very special group capable of a variety of tasks, mainly problem solving, requiring the ability to think 'outside the square'. However, there may be occasions when commando-type skills will have to be employed ... would you have the stomach and the ruthlessness required for such work?"

"I'd strangle Hitler with my bare hands, given the opportunity, Sir."

"No qualms about killing an enemy in close combat, Jeremy?"

"We're at war ... I'll carry out any order, Sir."

"Right, I'm sending you to Achnacarry, in the Highlands, for a full commando course. That's where you'll learn the hand-to-hand combat skills, the tricks of the trade. After that, have a week's leave and make the most of it because you're going to be very busy from then on. Oh, by the way, your soldier career from now on will be hush-hush, top secret. You can't tell family or friends the nature of your real duties. Is that understood?"

"Fully understood, Sir."

"Good, report back to me here after your leave."

❧

Jeremy was fully occupied in the highlands for three months, learning things which were foreign to his placid nature but apparently necessary to save his life if he ever found himself in a Commando-type situation. His physical fitness reached its peak on the route march over rough terrain, culminating in climbing to the peak of Ben Nevis.

At the conclusion of the course, he had never felt fitter or stronger in his life. Now, he looked forward to a spot of leave, catching up with the Lennox family and, most of all, with Grace Devine.

Jeremy's first port of call was CWS headquarters. Joe hugged him. "You look really well, Jeremy ... army life must suit you. Come through to my office and tell me all your news. I see you're an officer already ... Captain, if I'm not mistaken?"

"Yes, Joe, they put me in the Signals Corps."

"Well, they are the boys who are always in the front line, organising communication. I'm surprised ... I imagined you in a role more suited to your education, one of those back-room boys, you know, part of the think tank?"

"As it happens, Joe, I don't think I'm going to be in the front line ... I'm adjutant to a Colonel in the Ministry of Defence, a pretty cushy job ... not at all what I signed up for."

"Just what does an adjutant do?"

"I go everywhere the Colonel goes. I take the minutes at meetings and present him with a full report of the proceedings. I am really his administrative assistant, doing all the legwork to make sure things get done. That's about it, Joe ... not much danger there."

"Well, I'm pleased to hear that and I'm sure Jean will be too. Have you seen Grace yet?"

"Not yet ... actually, Joe, I was hoping to borrow a company car for a week, to take Grace on a wee holiday."

"You can ... you're still on the books as an employee. The schools are in recess, so she'll be free to go with you. Before you set off though, you must bring her to dinner tonight ... is that OK?"

"That'll be great ... will all the kids be there?"

"They will, Jeremy. Actually, I'd like you to have a private word with young Jim. There's something troubling him but ... well, he's a deep thinker and keeps himself to himself. I can't get through to him, too old, I guess. Perhaps he'll talk to you ... would you mind?"

"Not at all, Joe. I'll do what I can. Now, I'd better make sure Grace is available for tonight. Can I ring her from here?"

"Sure, help yourself ... I'll see you later around 6 o'clock."

Jeremy met Grace at her flat just as she was waving goodbye to one of her piano students. He lifted her and carried her across the threshold back into the flat. She laughed, saying "I hope none of the neighbours saw that, Jem. A handsome army officer being unduly familiar. What will they think?"

"Who cares?" said Jeremy, as he kissed her passionately. "I've missed you so much, Grace. I feel as if we should be married."

"I missed you too, Jem, but we've discussed the marriage thing. Have you changed your mind about waiting?"

Jeremy sighed, "No, not really, we have to be sensible, I suppose."

"I'm looking forward to this wee holiday you've planned. Where are you taking me?"

"Oh, we'll just head for the highlands and stop wherever we feel like, Grace."

"How romantic, but ... heavens, look at the time ... we'd better get to Jean's place."

"Jeremy, Jeremy, just look at you," said Jean, hugging him close. "My, it's grand to see you. Joe tells me you've landed yourself a cushy job in London. I'm real pleased about that. Come on in, the pair of you, dinner awaits."

Jeremy smiled and nodded at the two boys, waiting patiently for their dinner.

"How are things at school, boys?"

"I'm finished school, Jeremy," said Alec, "I start an aeronautical course at uni after the summer break."

"That's great news, Alec ... flying has always been your thing, right?"

"I'll say ... I've joined the Air Training Corps and am learning to fly in a flight simulator. It's exciting ... by the time I join up, it won't take me long to get my wings. I can't wait, Jeremy."

"Ah well, it'll come soon enough," said Jeremy, glancing at Jim, sitting quietly with his head down. "Now, your mum's calling us to shut up and eat. Good advice ... come on, I'm starving."

After partaking of Jean's delicious cuisine, Grace, Wee Kate, and Jean cleared the table and went to the kitchen to wash the dishes. Young Jim retired to his room, leaving Joe and Jeremy to hear more of Alec's enthusiastic plans.

At the first opportunity, Jeremy excused himself to have his promised talk with young Jim. He knocked on the bedroom door, "It's Jeremy here, Jim ... can I come in for a minute?"

"Come in, Jeremy ... is there something wrong?"

"No, son, nothing wrong ... it's just that your brother commandeered the conversation earlier, so I just wanted to catch up with you. I take it you don't share his enthusiasm for the air force?"

"Far from it ... I hate the whole idea of killing people, Jeremy."

"Me too, Jim ... I just wish it didn't have to be."

"I don't understand ... Joe told me you volunteered ... why?"

"Before I answer that, what will you do in a couple of years, when you are conscripted?"

"Oh, Christ, Jeremy, I don't know. I've been reading the history of the American Civil War. Jesus, what carnage, brother against brother ... it all seemed so pointless. If this war's still on when they call me up, I may register as a conscientious objector. Well, there you have it, you probably think I'm just a coward."

"On the contrary, son, it takes a special kind of courage to be a pacifist in wartime. This may surprise you but, when I was your age, my thinking was similar to yours."

"Really? What changed your mind?"

"In my final year at university, I became friendly with a Jewish lecturer who told me that he was a political refugee from Nazi Germany. He told me about the rise to power of Adolf Hitler and the beginning of Fascism in the country."

"What do you mean by Fascism, Jeremy?"

"It is a political system which denies people basic human rights. Hitler used military power to enforce the system, incarcerating anyone who dared advocate opposing views. He has embarked on a campaign of ethnic cleansing, herding Jews into ghettos as a precursor to packing them off to concentration camps."

"That sounds horrible ... surely the normal German people didn't approve of all that."

"Hitler has a massive propaganda machine feeding his patriotic fervour daily to the masses. The people are told that the avaricious Jews were responsible for the country's economic woes before Herr Hitler took over. Now, the aim is to create the master race, free of Jews, Slavs, gypsies, and other types regarded as sub-human."

"Jesus, Jeremy, how come I haven't heard a word about all that stuff until now?"

"I'm afraid we were more interested in overseas trade and increasing Britain's wealth so that we could enjoy a better lifestyle. In the meantime, Hitler was re- arming at an unprecedented rate. Now, he is set on world dominance and, this is my point, Jim, he has got to be stopped. That is what changed my mind. I'd sooner lose my life defending my country than live under the Nazi jackboot. Now, do you understand, son?"

"Yes, Jeremy, I understand your decision ... my problem is that, regardless of the enemy's behaviour, I just wouldn't have the aggression in me to kill anyone."

"Well, at least you realise that ... lots of people don't really know how they'll react until they're faced with the situation. Tell me, Jim, what career do you have in mind?"

"Until recently, I had no idea but, after reading about the horrible injuries incurred in wars, I'd really like to study medicine. Saving lives rather than taking them ... that's my ambition."

"Have you told Joe or your mum about this, son?"

"No, Jeremy, Joe has been very good to us and I'm grateful but I'd be loath to pressure him beyond his means. A university course in medicine is long and costly ... I wouldn't want to embarrass him ... do you know what I mean?"

"You know, Jim, for a teenager, you have sensitivity well beyond your years. I admire that. Look, I wouldn't be worried about Joe's financial situation. However, I do understand that you'd like to be independent as soon as possible and I'm sure you will achieve that before long. Joe tells me that you are much more gifted academically than Alec. If I were in your shoes now, I'd be telling the school principal of your ambitions so that he can select the most suitable subjects over the next two years. Then, if you applied yourself, which I know you will, I'm certain that you'll win a scholarship towards a medical degree."

"You're showing a deal of confidence in me, Jeremy, but that whole scenario will come crashing down if I refuse to fight, won't it?"

"No son, you'll have another option as a medical student. When you turn 18, rather than wait to be called up, you could volunteer to join the Royal Army Medical Corps. You wouldn't have to carry a gun ... most likely you'd be carrying a stretcher. You'll be at the front, risking your life like the troops but doing your bit to bring down Hitler without sacrificing your principles. How does that sound to you, Jim?"

"It sounds a whole lot better than what I had in mind. I'm glad we had this talk, Jeremy. I've been in a dark place but you've opened a window and let the sunshine in. Now, I won't have to worry my family about my pacifism. I thank you and I'll go along with your advice."

"Good, son ... what has happened in this room stays in this room but, when you get the chance, tell Joe of your ambition to be a doctor ... no more, no less. I can assure you he'll be over the moon. Now, Jim, as you've cheered up considerably, let's go downstairs ... I want to hear young Kate playing the piano."

Chapter 11

Jeremy Cowan and Grace Devine,
Irrevocably committed 'ere he leaves for the line.

Following a pleasant evening, Joe escorted Grace and Jeremy to the front gate. "Jeremy, did you manage to have a word with young Jim?"

"Yes, I did, Joe, and everything's sorted. You don't have to worry about him now."

"Thanks, Jeremy, he certainly looks a lot happier now. Anyway, I won't hold you up. Good night to the pair of you and I hope you have a nice trip."

As he drove Grace home, Jeremy said, "I'm going to Gilmorehill now to pack for our wee trip, my love, but the way I feel right now I'd sooner be staying here with you."

"Oh Jem, there's nothing I'd like better but my flatmate is a teacher at the Catholic school so ..."

"I understand, love ... look, I'll pick you up at 9.30 in the morning and then we can head off, far from the madding crowd."

She kissed him passionately and murmured, "Don't be late, my love."

Jeremy had already informed the council that he was ending his tenancy. Apart from some books, all he had to pack was clothing. So, after a good night's sleep, he was ready to leave.

Grace came out as he arrived on time. "Let's go, Jem ... I can't wait to see a bit of the highlands. I've read about my native land but never had the chance to explore it."

As she sat in the car, she leaned across and kissed him. "I promise to keep my hands off you today but tonight, a different kind of exploration will happen."

"That's nice to know, my love ... perhaps we'll finish sightseeing by lunchtime. However, let's get to Drymen quickly ... I've had no breakfast."

"Nor I, Jem, I was too excited to eat."

At the pretty little village of Drymen, they enjoyed a hearty breakfast, after which they drove to Balmaha, where Grace had her first look at the famous Loch Lomond. They drove the entire length of the loch and turned right to the Trossachs. Soon they skirted Loch Katrine. Jeremy said, "This is the source of the pure water which the Glasgow people enjoy."

"Oh, Jem, this is all so pretty ... how can anyone ever emigrate and leave all this beauty behind?"

"Mostly for economic reasons, Grace ... a better life and more opportunities for their children."

"Jem, let's take a walk through the heather ... I don't want to leave this spot for a while."

They reached a secluded glade and Grace lay down, pulling Jeremy towards her. "Come, darling, let's consummate our relationship right here ... I can't wait any longer."

"Oh Grace, I don't have any contraceptives ... I'll buy some when we get to Callander."

"Relax, darling, we don't need them. As it happens, this is the safe time of the month for me. As a Catholic, I learned all about the rhythm method, endorsed by the Church."

"Are you sure, Grace ... I don't want to go off to war, leaving you an unmarried mother."

"I'm sure, darling ... now, come on, relax and let's enjoy this."

Later, resuming their journey, Grace said happily, "Now I can really appreciate this wonderful scenery ... Jem, the Trossachs must be the most beautiful spot in the world."

Jeremy laughed, "There are lots of travel writers who would agree with you. You know, lass, that unexpected exercise back there has whetted my appetite for a good feed. We'll book into the best hotel in Callander for dinner, bed and breakfast. How does that sound, Grace?"

"Lovely, Jem ... see if the bridal suite is available. My appetite is also whetted for more of the same. I want to have my wicked way with you."

"Christ, Grace, I may have caught a tigress by the tail here."

"Oh, please don't tell me I'm too much for you, Jem."

"I think I'll be able to accommodate you, my love," he replied, musing that the commando training may be useful in more ways than one.

A few days and nights of blissful companionship cemented the love of two people, overcoming the elephant in the room ... the realisation that they would soon be parted for God knows how long.

On their last evening in the Callander Hotel, after they had dined early, Jeremy said, "Grace, I'd love to hear you on that grand piano and I'm sure the other guests would appreciate your playing ... would you mind, darling?"

"What would you like to hear, Jem?"

"Your choice, my love ... I just want to hear your exquisite soft touch."

"Mm, I think you may have had enough of my soft touch, sweetheart."

"Never, Grace ... now come on, surprise me."

Grace quietly made her way to the Steinway piano, surprised to find such a prestigious instrument in a small town in the highlands of Scotland. She began to doodle on the piano, undecided what to play for her lover.

The maitre d' approached Grace and she rose, expecting him to ask her to return to her seat. "No, no, please don't go ... could you play some nice dance music?"

Grace smiled, nodded, and began to play, in foxtrot tempo, 'I'm Confessin'. To her delight, a few couples rose and responded to her rhythm. Soon, the small dance floor was filled with diners, obviously enjoying her performance.

Jeremy looked on, immensely proud of her. However, the best was yet to come. Grace looked directly at him and began to sing in a sexy, husky voice. This came as a complete surprise ... he had no idea she could sing, especially in such a seductive manner. As she finished, there was loud applause and shouts of encore.

Grace looked at Jeremy enquiringly. When he gave her the thumbs-up she shrugged and launched into a medley of songs, ideally suited to after-dinner entertainment ... 'As Time Goes By', 'A Nightingale sang in Berkeley Square', 'These Foolish Things', etc.

At 10pm, the manager announced, "Unfortunately, ladies and gentlemen, there is a war on and we have to close now. Our regular pianist has been called up and is now serving in the navy but, I think we should thank this lady for standing in and providing such wonderful entertainment."

Everyone stood and applauded enthusiastically until they were asked to leave.

When they stood to retire to their room, the manager thanked Grace personally. "As a jazz fan, I reckon you are the nearest voice to Billie Holiday I've ever heard. Are you familiar with her work?"

"As a fellow jazz fan," said Grace, "who hasn't heard of Lady Day?"

"Well, I don't know what your plans are in these uncertain times but let me just say that you will always be welcome here and as a mark of my gratitude, your bill will be waived."

Back in their room, Jeremy said, "My God, Grace, you were wonderful. Why haven't you mentioned that you could sing like that?"

"Jem, I've never sung seriously in my life. The only reason I sang this evening was that you looked so forlorn, at the table on your own ... I only sang for you. Couldn't you tell? ... I was looking straight at you."

"Ultimately, I got the message, darling, and it made me realise just how much you've come to mean to me. I want to spend the rest of my life with you but there's something I have to tell you."

"Oh, Jem, please don't tell me you have a wife somewhere already."

"No, no, my love, it's nothing like that. It's to do with my army job."

"What do you mean, Jem? You told me you had a cushy job, babysitting some damn Colonel ... wasn't that the truth?"

"It's true, Grace, for the time being, and that's what I wanted Jean to believe but, when I get back to London, the Colonel has other plans for me. Now, I can't tell you more because I'm sworn to secrecy. I'm telling you this now because I probably won't be seeing you or writing to you for … well, for God knows how long. I've nominated you as my next of kin, in case … well, you know what. So, as long as you don't receive any official notification from the War Office, you can assume I'm OK."

"Jem, I never believed for one moment that story you concocted for Jean's peace of mind. Never underestimate me again, darling."

"Joe Lennox told me a while back how strong you are. So, my love, where do we go from here?"

"Well, sweetheart, isn't it obvious … let's go to bed and make this a night to remember."

Chapter 12

Behind the lines in occupied France,
Jem helps lead the Hun a merry dance.

*J*eremy reported to Colonel Nicholson on arrival at the Ministry of Defence. "Ah, welcome back, Jeremy. I trust you had an enjoyable leave."

"Yes, thank you, Sir."

"I've had excellent reports about your performance at Achnacarry. The Commando chief was most reluctant to see you go ... he wants you transferred to his group but I have other plans for you. You are now officially part of Strategic Services, which covers a multitude of sins."

"What does that really mean, Sir?"

"Basically, Jeremy, our group has to be multi-skilled, innovative, with the acumen to think out a solution to any problem and the ability to implement it."

"But, I'm not exactly multi-skilled, Sir."

"Not yet, but you will be. You've done the Commando bit and your university qualifications show that you can think for yourself. Now, do you know Morse Code, by any chance?"

"Oh, I know what it is ... I've played around with it years ago, just for fun."

"Good ... I'm now going to send you round to Baker Street for a crash training course on Morse Code and the latest wireless transceiver equipment ... just another skill you may need later. I reckon you'll be au fait with that stuff from an operational standpoint in a week or less. When you report back, I'll have a real job for you."

Five days later, Jeremy again reported to Colonel Nicholson. "I'm up to date with Morse Code now, Sir. They've given me two of the latest wireless transceiver equipment ... very impressive, Sir, it doesn't take up much room."

"Good, Jeremy ... you know of course about the British Expeditionary Force?"

"Yes Sir, the BEF, a large British army contingent, now in France, supporting our allies."

"That's correct and, from all reports, the French are going to need all the help we can give them."

"Yes, Sir ... what do you want me to do?"

"I want you to go to France and meet Major Mike Ferguson of Royal Signals. You'll be flown you to Calais, where he'll pick you up and drive you south to where the BEF spearhead is located at present. He's a fellow Scot so you won't have any trouble with the language. That's a joke, Jeremy but he does speak fluent French, which will be a great asset for the job in hand."

"What exactly is my job over there, Sir?"

"Ferguson will give you all the gen. Take those wireless transceivers with you ... that's essential. I'm promoting you to Major so you'll be on equal footing with Ferguson. Any questions, Jeremy?"

"No, Sir."

"Good, off you go and pack a few essentials. Tomorrow morning early, you'll be picked up and taken to Hendon aerodrome. There will be a pilot waiting for you ... Good luck."

On arrival at Calais next morning, he was greeted by Major Ferguson. "Welcome to France, I'm Mike Ferguson."

"Thanks, Mike, I'm Jeremy Cowan, Jem for short."

"A fellow Scot ... which part do you hail from, Jem?"

"Glasgow ... and you?"

"I was born in Stirling but my old man got a job transfer to France when I was 11, so my higher education was in Amiens."

"Colonel Nicholson told me you spoke fluent French. He also said you'd fill me in on my role here."

"That's right, Jem, I speak a bit of German too, but let's get going ... I'll tell you all about it on the way."

As they sped south, Mike said, "Our guys are spread out along a line about 10 kilometres north of Amiens, my old town. We're in hilly forest country and that may be the problem, Jem."

"What's the problem, Mike?"

"Communication ... the wireless transceivers we have keep cutting out, especially in the armoured cars and the few tanks we have. They're unreliable in this terrain. Your job is to install one of the latest jobs in a vehicle and train the operator. The second unit you'll set up at H/Q where we're heading now. It's a place in the mountains used for specialist forces training ... like our commando camps back home. Are you familiar with them, Jem?"

"I sure am. I did the full commando course in the Scottish Highlands."

"Is that right? Well, laddie, you're not just a back-room boy, are you?"

"No, Mike, strategic services, but I can't tell you much more."

"Still," said Mike, "I'm glad you told me that much. I'll introduce you to an old school friend of mine when we arrive ... I fancy you'll have a lot in common."

"Henri, I'd like you to meet Jem Cowan. Jem, this is Henri Montand ... he runs the commando school here and he speaks better English than we do."

"Hi, Jem ... we don't call it a commando school, simply Special Services, but I guess we do the same stuff. Are you a commando?"

"No, Henri, I did all the training but my boss had other ideas for me."

"So, what's your line of business, my friend?"

"A little bit of everything, Henri ... you could say we're flexible, just do what's required when it's required."

"Stick around, Henri," said Mike, "Jem has the latest thing in communication. He's going to set it up and contact his boss in London. Meanwhile, let's you and I have a drink ... you're off-duty at the moment, aren't you?"

"Yes, Mike, and I have some old cognac in my quarters. I've been keeping it for a special occasion, so what's more special than seeing my old school friend again?"

The two friends relaxed over a couple of glasses of fine French liquor. "How's your sister, Henri? I suppose she's married now?"

"Yvette is in the pink, as you Brits say. She's still single, Mike, a bit of a workaholic. She's the doctor in charge of a small clinic in Amiens. She'd love to see you, Mike, I'm sure ... will you have time to visit?"

"I'll make time when our mob advances to Amiens ... I was very fond of Yvette in the old days. In a way, I was sorry when my father transferred back to England. I was 17 then. A year later, I joined the army and now I'm back in France as a Major. I learned of your whereabouts before I left England. You see, I'm not really part of our expeditionary force ... I, too, am in a kind of special branch, answering to the Foreign Office, which seems to have access to all kinds of information. My job is to be an observer, reporting any new or unexpected activities over here. Now, mon ami, put the cork back in that special bottle and let's find out how Jem's getting on."

They didn't have long to wait as Jem burst into the room. "Guys, I've got some big news for you. Is there any chance of getting a slug out of that bottle you're corking up?"

"Certainly, Jem, I think Mike and I will have another drink too ... it looks like we're going to need it," said Henri. "Here you are, Jem ... now, what's your news?"

Jem drained his glass and said, "My boss has just informed me that France is on the point of surrendering to the Germans. The BEF is going to be withdrawn right away. The German army has control of Calais, so the

British forces have been ordered to get to the port of Dunkirk as soon as possible. They are caught in a pincer movement from east and west. Soon, Amiens will be next to fall and the Huns will be harassing the Brits from the south as well. Our troops will be battling the odds to get away."

"Jesus," exploded Mike, "what are your orders, Jem?"

"The Colonel will get back to me as soon as the surrender is confirmed. Now, what will you guys do?"

"Well, our government may surrender," said Henri, "but I have no intention of meekly giving in to *les Boches*. I have 20 young guys in training here and I'll guarantee they'll side with me. We'll form a resistance group here in the mountains. This is an ideal spot ... it's well off the beaten track and the Germans don't know of its existence."

"That's true and I'll join you," said Mike, "that's what the British Foreign Office would want me to do. It's the perfect spot for a bit of guerrilla warfare."

"Right," said Jem, "let's go across to my transceiver. I'm not going to wait for the Colonel's call ... I'm going to call him and tell him I want to join you guys ... I'm sure he'll agree. When I tell him the set-up and the number of French commandos here, he'll enthuse about it. This is the sort of situation he recruited me for."

"Jem," said Henri, "ask your boss if he knows when Amiens is going to be occupied by the Nazis. That's important ... I'll tell you why later, but let's hurry now."

"Right, guys," said Jem, "It's been confirmed ... the French government has surrendered. Marshal Petain now heads a government, headquartered in the town of Vichy, in Southern France, the unoccupied zone. Unfortunately, this Vichy France is a German ally. Now, as I forecast, Colonel Nicholson is in full agreement that I should remain here. I'll be the contact between him and Henri. He forecasts that, if we're going to be really useful, we'll going to need arms and ammunition. To that end, we'll have to mark out with flares an area where a Hudson can drop supplies by parachute. Later on, we should mark out a short landing strip for a Lysander, in case the Colonel wants to plant a German-speaking agent over here."

"Did you find out about Amiens, Jem?"

"Yes, Henri, the Jerries will be there in 36 hours."

"Good, that gives us time to collect all the arms and ammunitions from the French army dump there. I'll take half a dozen men in a truck, load up, and bring the stuff back here. I'm leaving nothing for the Huns."

"I'll come with you, if I may," said Mike, "I'd love to see Yvette."

"Good idea, Mike ... my sister will be pleased to see you. We'll drop you off at the clinic on the way to the dump and pick you up on the way back."

Mike spotted Yvette as soon as he entered the clinic and his heart momentarily stopped, missing a beat at the vision of loveliness. He realised that, despite the intervening years, he was still in love with her. Although he was aware that she could speak English, he thought it expedient to speak French.

"How are you, Yvette?"

She looked up from a patient, in surprise, "Michael, where on earth did you spring from?"

"It's a long story ... can you spare time to listen?"

"Of course, come to my office."

As soon as they reached the office, she came into his arms, kissing him passionately. "Oh, Michael, Michael, I thought I'd never see you again. So much has happened and now we're at war ... is that why you're here in France?"

"Yvette, when we parted, we were innocent teenagers, but I loved you then. I love you even more now, as a mature adult. There has never been anyone else in my life, darling."

"That goes for me too, my Michael. I buried myself in work and study. Now, I'm in charge of this 20-bed clinic, determined to devote myself to my career, with no thought of marriage. Now, you've appeared, out of the blue, and my head is in a whirl ... I am unable to think straight."

"Have you heard that your government has surrendered to the Germans?"

"No, but I can't say I'm surprised. Les Boches seem to be too well armed and Herr Hitler has ambitions to dominate all of Europe."

"Well, your brother is going to fight on, Yvette. He has organised a resistance group and I am part of it. The Germans will be in Amiens about 36 hours from now. Our group intends to hide out in the hills. As we speak, Henri is filling a truck with arms and ammunition from the local army depot. He'll be here within the hour to collect me."

"Oh, God, Michael, I've just found you only to lose you again."

"You could come with me if you like. You'd be safe in the hills until I can get you to England."

"I can't leave here, Michael ... I have patients here who depend on me for their well-being. Anyway, I'll be safe here ... even the Germans will realise my importance in the community. Your offer is tempting but I have a duty of care here, you understand."

"Yes, darling, it was wishful thinking on my part ... I knew what your response would be. Still, I hate the thought of leaving you again."

"The end of this damned war could be years away but what can we do, Michael?"

"I've just thought of a way for us to be together. I could live here as a handyman, in your employ. I could be the eyes and ears for your brother as part of the community ... if you're agreeable, we'll talk it over with Henri."

"But would you be safe, Michael ... it sounds very dangerous?"

"Darling, it's what I've been trained to do ... I speak fluent French and I understand German. The Huns will assume I'm a local man."

"They may be suspicious of a fit-looking specimen like you not being in the army, Michael."

"Well, darling, perhaps you can help there with some illness making me unfit for service."

"Yes, I can say you've been diagnosed with leukaemia ... early stages but terminal in the medium term. You're my patient but happy to work for your keep as long as you're able."

"Excuse my ignorance, Yvette, what is this illness? I suppose I ought to know a bit about it, if I'm asked."

Yvette laughed, "Yes, my love, it might be expedient. You have blood cancer and I'm keeping it at bay with regular blood transfusions."

As the couple smiled lovingly at each other, Henri arrived. "I can see you two are still friends despite the years apart."

Yvette embraced her brother. "Yes, Henri, but we are more than friends and want to be together. Michael has a proposition for you to consider."

Mike quickly outlined the plan and Henri immediately realised the benefit of having a man on the spot.

"That's great, Mike ... I have enough commandos on board. You'll be much more useful here. You'll be able to communicate with Jem if we give you the spare transceiver. Come back with me now ... Jem will train you on the transceiver and you can bring it back here. We have a motor-cycle at the camp. Can you ride a motor-cycle?"

"Yes, and I know Morse Code, so I can be back here quickly to get organised. I have a good feeling about this, Henri."

"Yes, Mike," said Henri, smiling at his sister, "you'll have the best of both worlds."

Chapter 13

Scotland

The rhythm method fails the test
And Mother Nature does the rest.

*T*owards the end of January, 1940, Grace called in after school to see Jean. "Hello, Grace, have you had a letter from Jeremy yet?"

"No, Jean, but I'm not really expecting one. He warned me just before he left that he was going off on some special job and wouldn't be in touch for a while. I'm OK with that but an unexpected problem has come up ... that's what I want to talk to you about."

"Well, lass, you and Jeremy are like family to me, so problems will be shared. Joe always says that there are no problems, only solutions, so tell me what's worrying you."

"Oh, Jean, I feel embarrassed ... I've missed two periods and I'm pretty sure I'm pregnant. When Jeremy and I were on that trip to the highlands, I miscalculated, outsmarted myself, and this is the result."

Jean laughed, "Well, congratulations, Grace, you're going to be a mammy and Jeremy will have a pleasant surprise when he comes home on leave. There you are, I couldn't be happier for you."

"Ah, Jean, you're forgetting where I'm teaching. In another month or so, I'll start to show and questions will be asked by the school board. I'm not going to wait for the inquisition ... I'll give notice before that happens and find another place to live."

"Grace, Grace, Grace, give notice now and come and live here with us."

"That's a generous offer, Jean, but that wouldn't be fair on the rest of your family. No, I'll have to think of another answer."

"Well, here comes Joe, the solution finder himself ... let's ask his advice."

Grace cringed in embarrassment as Jean told Joe the situation. When Jean finished, Joe went to the drinks cupboard and poured himself a glass of Scotch, saying, "Jean doesn't drink and from now on you can't drink, Grace, so that leaves me to do the honours."

He raised his glass and offered congratulations to the mother-to-be and the absent Jeremy. "Grace, I will brook no argument ... you will come here as a welcome part of this family. I couldn't be happier. To avoid being conscripted, you will continue officially as a teacher after the birth of your baby.

"I'm very happy too," said Jean, "I'm home on my own all day, Grace. You'll be great company for me and you can help me in the kitchen. If you're worried about money, you can pay for your keep by extra tutoring Kate on the piano. She'll be delighted, lass ... she just lives for your visits. So, you agree, solution found?"

"Yes, Jean, solution found."

A month later, Grace was ensconced as part of the Lennox family. Alec had turned 17 and was an engineering student at Glasgow university. He was also a keen member of the university's Air Training Corps, so she didn't see much of him.

Young Jim was still at Allan Glen's school, taking extra courses as required to get him a scholarship to study medicine at the uni. He came home with Joe every day and was always anxious to talk to her, to find out any news of Jeremy.

It became obvious to Grace that Jim idolized Jeremy but she didn't know why.

Kate was almost 10 years old and took advantage, unashamedly, of Grace's presence, so keen was she to master the piano.

Assisted by the local midwife and Jean, Grace gave birth to a healthy baby girl on July 4th, 1940. It had been an easy pregnancy and home birth and Grace was up and about in no time.

On Friday evening, the entire family was gathered at the dinner table. Young Alec said, somewhat dubiously, "What a pity Jeremy's not here, Grace ... I trust he's in good health, wherever he is."

"As do I, Alec ... hope springs eternal in the human breast."

"Oh, Grace, that's lovely," said Jean, "did you just make that up?"

"No, Jean," said Grace, "I'm not sure but I think Burns wrote it."

Young Jim spoke up, "Actually it's part of a verse from the Essay on Man, by Alexander Pope."

Joe beamed at Jim, "Do you know the rest of the verse, Jim?"

"I think so," said Jim.

> *Hope springs eternal in the human breast;*
> *Man never is, but always to be blest;*
> *The soul, uneasy and confined from home,*
> *Rests and expatiates in a life to come.*

"Thank you, Jim," said Joe, "it's nice to have a classical scholar in the family."

"We're studying Pope at school at present and that verse intrigues me. I'm certain that Jeremy will, one day soon, come home to Grace and their child."

Grace nodded at Jim, thinking, "Jeremy obviously has influenced this boy in a good way. We'll find out what, in due course."

"Have you decided on a name for the bairn yet, Grace?" said Jean.

"Well, after hearing young Jim's recitation, there's only one name possible," said Grace.

"And what would that be, lass?"

"Hope, of course ... Hope Cowan."

Chapter 14

Alec MacDonald joins the band
Of heroes in the Fighter Command

A year later, Alec, on his 18th birthday, volunteered for flying duties in the RAF. With his background, he was accepted and immediately sent to basic training, following which he was sent to flying school. After completing his first solo flight in a Spitfire, he was posted to Tangmere airfield, near the south coast of England, where he was immediately dubbed Mac by all and sundry.

The Battle of Britain had been well and truly won in 1940 and Fighter Command was used mainly as escorts for Bomber Command on their raids on German cities.

A big problem was the limited range of the Spitfire and the Hurricane fighters.

This meant that on distant targets, the escort fighters had to turn for home prematurely, leaving the bombers to defend themselves against the Messerschmitt fighters when over the target.

This frustrated Alec but, when his squadron leader gave the order to return, there was no option but to obey.

Over the next two years, however, he had his share of successes, shooting down 5 Messerschmitt ME110s over the English Channel. He longed for the day when the designers could produce a long-range fighter.

By this time, he now had the rank of squadron leader and on his 60th escort mission, over Hamburg, he issued the order to his group to head for home. As he waited and watched his charges obeying his command, he noticed a solitary ME110 on his tail. He immediately took evasive action and, following some skilful aerobatics, managed to turn the tables on the German and shot him down. Unfortunately, he was now desperately low on fuel and, after safely passing over the German-occupied Channel Islands, he was reading on empty. He radioed base, "Mac calling base, over."

"Come in, Mac, you're late. Are you in trouble? Over."

"Yes, I've just run out of fuel. I'm about 1o miles out from Dover and gradually losing height. I'll try to glide as close as possible to the White Cliffs. With a bit of luck, I'll still have enough height to get over them and land in the nearest field. Over."

"Good luck, Mac ... keep us posted. Over."

"Will do ... over and out."

As he approached the White Cliffs, Alec could see he did not have the height to glide over them. "Mac, calling base, over."

"Come in, Mac, what is your position? Over."

"Not enough height to get over ... banking left now ... will try to ditch as close as possible to the cliff face. Oh, this is a bit tricky ..."

As he tried to land in the shallows, he struck rocks and capsized, losing consciousness.

The base officer heard the collision and the line was dead. "Come in, Mac, over." He realised it was fruitless, looked at his superior officer and shook his head.

On top of the cliffs, an official observer witnessed the entire incident and reported it to the authorities. A rescue boat was quickly despatched from Dover to the scene and Alec was stretchered to hospital, alive, but still unconscious.

He came to on arriving at the hospital and was in agony. He was heavily sedated before being examined by the emergency doctor. His injuries included a fractured skull, fractured clavicle, broken tibia, and two broken ankles. "This chap's lucky to be alive. He must have been pretty fit to survive this lot ... let's get him to theatre straight away, Sister."

After all the operations had been carried out, Squadron Leader MacDonald was transferred to the rehab wing at Chichester, conveniently close to Tangmere airfield, so his fellow pilots were able to visit him when off duty.

He telephoned home and his mother answered the phone. "Hello, Mum, Alec here."

"Hello, son, it's lovely to hear your voice ... are you well?"

"Yes, Mum, I had a wee bit of trouble but I'm getting better. I'm in rehabilitation in Chichester hospital and will be here for a while."

"Oh, my God, what happened, Alec? Did you crash? Are you burnt? Tell me, son!"

"Don't worry, Mum ... Look, I had a dodgy landing and broke a leg ... my own fault. It's fixed now ... I just have to exercise it every day until the doc gives me the all-clear. Now, how are things at home?"

"Everybody's fine, son ... a wee bit of news, your brother joined up and is in the Royal Army Medical Corps. Is there any chance of you getting leave soon? We'd love to see you, Alec."

"There's every chance, Mum, but not before I've finished in rehab. I'll keep you posted ... listen, the doctor has just arrived, so I'll have to hang up. I'll see you soon."

Alec spent Christmas in rehab and returned to Tangmere on January 3rd, 1944. He reported to Wing Commander Hammond. "Ah, Mac, fit and well now, I gather?"

"Yes sir, rarin' to go. Have you a new Spitfire for me?"

"Negative, Mac, I've something different in mind for you ... no more Spitfires. You were always complaining about them anyway."

"Oh, please, please, not ground duties, Sir. Look, I loved the Spits ... my only complaint was their range limitation. I want to get back in the air, Sir."

"Relax, Mac ... you're going on a course on the latest Mosquito fighter/bomber. It's the fastest thing in the air ... it will outpace Jerry's new Messerschmitt **and** no more range problems."

"Oh, that's a relief, Sir, I thought you'd lost faith in me."

"Come off it, Mac, we all know you're the best fighter pilot Tangmere's ever had. First though, you're going to have two weeks leave. There will be a squadron of Mosquitos here when you get back. You'll be in the air soon enough."

As it happened, Alec's leave was cancelled. Some undisclosed emergency had cropped up and he was sent to Biggin Hill to have a crash course on the Mosquito.

In Amiens, Mike had settled into his new role. In the evenings, he frequented the popular cafes and taverns, sitting quietly, obsequiously becoming part of the local scene. He listened to the German officers, in particular, hoping to glean information which could be helpful to Henri. Over time, he had passed info about the transport of supplies and the like to the resistance and Henri's commandos had made successful sorties as a result.

On one auspicious evening Mike had learned that around 100 resistance fighters from the south had been captured and imprisoned in Amiens jail. Later, he overheard two prison guards discussing the impending execution of the resistance men. The date scheduled was February 19th, a month hence. Mike relayed the details to Jem, who duly forwarded the message to Colonel Nicholson in London.

Chapter 15

Biggin Hill

Alec joins a special fleet
Of Mosquito pilots, all elite.

The pilots assembled at Biggin Hill were the best available in the entire country for an important task. Wing Commander Pickford addressed them:

"Gentlemen, the job ahead of you calls for the highest skills. When you are fully acquainted with the Mosquito fighter/bomber, you will fly to a remote location in Scotland. There, for the next two weeks, you will practise high-speed, low-level bombing. Your bombs will have a set delay of 5 seconds following release, to offer enough time to get away without damage from the explosions. I shall be in charge and will order consecutive attacks on the same target when safe to do so. Now, as you can imagine, even these practice runs carry a degree of danger ... any questions?"

"What's the target, Sir?" asked Squadron Leader MacDonald."

"That's hush-hush at the moment, Mac. The element of surprise will be paramount ... we cannot take risks with security. You will be given all the info you need in plenty of time."

Two weeks passed without a hitch. The wing-commander praised his charges, declaring the crews to be the cream of RAF personnel, absolutely necessary for the coming mission. He told them that the target details would be revealed on their return to Biggin Hill.

It was decided that the elite crews be given two days leave to rest up and be 100% fit for the job ahead.

On their return, they were informed that their job was coded Operation Jericho.

Chapter 16

Amiens

Joshua fit the battle of Jericho
And the walls came tumbling down.

On February 16th, Jem received a message from Colonel Nicholson.

After decoding, Jem was pleased that action had been taken on the information provided by Mike with regard to the impending execution of the resistance fighters.

The prison walls will be breached in a low-level bombing attack on February 18th in the middle of the day, when the prisoners would be taking their fresh air and exercise break. In the subsequent confusion, there would be a mass outbreak, hundreds of prisoners seizing the opportunity to escape. It is anticipated that the hundred or so resistance fighters would have the experience and the physical fitness to head for the woods. Your people should maintain a watching brief in the hills and endeavour to pick up as many escapees as possible.

Jem relayed the information to Mike, who suggested a couple of trucks to be positioned north of the prison early on the morning of the attack, on the edge of the woods, hopefully to pick up the first batch of the escapees and transport them swiftly to our base, while the Huns are still befuddled and disorganised.

The Mosquito fleet came in low and fast. Wing-Commander Pickford broke the radio silence, "Okay, Mac, you're first ... you know your target, get in and out and head for home."

Alec MacDonald's navigator and bomb aimer, Flight Sergeant Hector White, released their load of four bombs. Unfortunately, one bomb detonated early and their plane was rocked by the blast and struck in several places. The Mosquito dipped and Mac pulled hard on the joystick to clear the wall on the far side. He turned north and was relieved to find the plane responding perfectly. However, a glance at the instrument panel revealed his fuel levels dropping rapidly. "We're in trouble, Hec. We're too low to bail out ... I'll have to put her down quickly."

"Look, Mac, there's a clearing in the woods up ahead with what appears to be a runway of sorts."

"I see it, Hec ... hang on and pray that we can pull up in time before we run out of runway."

Even with full flaps, Alec sensed that it would need a miracle to stop the plane before it smashed into the woods.

Henri, in a truck at the edge of the woods, was startled to see an RAF plane flying fast and low overhead. He could hear the engines spluttering and realised the plane was in trouble. Henri quickly realised that the pilot was going to try to land on the makeshift runway, designed for Lysander aircraft, which could land on a threepenny bit, as Mike would say. As he turned the truck around, he heard the almighty crash and hurried to the runway, although he did not expect to find anyone surviving.

He parked the truck at the end of the runway and saw that the plane had been smashed to smithereens. He was surprised to discover that most of the plane had been made of wood. There were two men lying prone on the ground. The first man was obviously dead, having been almost decapitated, probably by a tree branch. The other man was unconscious but breathing. Henri hoisted him on to his shoulder and placed him in the back of the truck.

Back at base, he laid the airman on a bed and went to Jem's office. "Jem, we have an injured RAF pilot unconscious. Can you send a signal to Mike and get him to bring my sister here quickly?"

Yvette arrived soon after with Mike. Henri was waiting for them and escorted them to the patient. Alec was still unconscious. "Strip him completely, boys", said Yvette, "he looks in a bad way."

Yvette had a smoke while the two men removed the airman's clothing.

"There you are, Sis, he's all yours," said Henri.

"My God, he's been through the mill," said Yvette. "There are bruises all over his body. I'm surprised he's still alive. OK, let me get down to business. He's had a bit of a blow to the head, He's still concussed, which is in his favour, because he also has a fractured clavicle. When he wakes up, he'll be in severe pain, so I propose to keep him under so that I can treat him."

Yvette got to work and later she told Henri, "This guy's been lucky ... surgery won't be necessary for either injury. I can see he has had a skull fracture in the recent past but this time, I cleaned the area of the blow, ensuring there was no infection. The clavicle will need to be supported for a while with a simple sling. When he comes to, he'll need pain killers for a while. Poor boy, the bruises to his body will get better in their own time. Until then, he'll need plenty of rest. Now, Michael, take me back to the clinic, and Henri, make sure you are with this young man when he comes to."

Alec woke up, disoriented, in pain. Gradually his eyes lost their blurriness and focused on the man standing at the foot of the bed. "Where am I? ... who are you?"

"You're in a French Resistance hideout. My name is Henri Montand, leader of the group here. When your plane crashed, I brought you here and your injuries have been treated. I wouldn't move quickly if I were you. You've been concussed and you have a fractured clavicle. That's why you have a sling. Now, what's your name?"

"Squadron Leader Alec MacDonald. Tell me, did you pick up my navigator too?"

"Yes, but I'm afraid he didn't survive the crash. What was his name, Alec?"

"Flight Sergeant Hector White. Oh, Christ, Hec bought it and yet I'm here, just banged up a wee bit ... there's no fuckin' justice."

"Bought it?" said Henri, "I don't understand."

"Sorry, mate, it's RAF slang for being killed in action. Are you guys in contact with the UK, by any chance?"

"Yes, Alec, I'll leave you for a few minutes and send over a guy who is in telegraphic communication with London, regularly. I can tell you're a Scot as he is, so he'll be able to communicate better than me. Do you want a pain-killer before I go?"

"No, mate, I can put up with a bit of discomfort so my brain stays alert."

As soon as Jem walked into the room, Alec exclaimed, "Jesus Christ!"

"Close, Alec, you got the initials right, JC."

"Jeremy Cowan, what the hell are you doing here?"

"Ah, Alec, thereby hangs a tale ... a long tale, too long to tell at the moment. Let's just say, I'm attached to the French Resistance."

"I see ... now I think I understand why you've been incommunicado for years. We thought you'd come to a bad end but Grace Devine was adamant that you were alive and well. You remember Grace, don't you, Jeremy?"

"Of course I do, Alec, she's the girl I'm going to marry when the war's over."

"Well, that's good to hear, Jeremy, because she's the mother of your daughter."

"My daughter! You're joking, aren't you, Alec? Grace assured me she wouldn't get pregnant."

"Accidents happen, mate. You have a beautiful little girl. Her name is Hope Cowan and everyone says she has your eyes."

"Jesus Christ, I'm flabbergasted ... she must be about four years old."

"That's right, and part of our family, along with Grace. Yes, they live with my mum and Joe. Jeremy, when you get over your shock, can you do something for me?"

"Of course, Alec, what do you need?"

"That French bloke, Henri, told me you are in regular contact with your people in London ... I need you to get word about Flight Sergeant Hector White, my navigator, killed in action, so his folks can be notified."

"No problem, Alec, and I'll inform my boss that you are injured but alive, in occupied France, out of action for a while."

"Good, Jeremy, is the medico who treated me here? I'd like to ask her when I'll be able to get up and about."

"No, Alec, she runs a clinic in Amiens. She'll only come here if urgently required. I reckon when the bruises ease off, you'll be able to move around. It may take a wee bit longer for the clavicle to knit, though."

"Fair enough, Jeremy, but as soon as possible I'd like to get back to my squadron. Is there any chance of that?"

"Sure, Alec, when you're ready, we can organise a Lysander to come across and get you back to the UK. Now, I'll go and contact London. When I come back, you can tell me more about Hope ... what a lovely name."

Chapter 17

Scotland

Alec's usually late arriving,
But an acknowledged expert at surviving.

*J*ean received a letter from the CO at Biggin Hill, informing her that Squadron Leader Alec MacDonald was alive and recovering from injuries received during a forced landing in France. He is being well looked after by a French resistance group and will be returning to the UK as soon as he is fit to travel.

Jean breathed a sigh of relief, having expected the worst kind of news on receiving the official letter. She shared the news with Grace and Kate and, when Joe came home, she had a private chat with him, admitting that she was concerned about Alec's safety, despite the CO's assurance that he was being well looked after. "Joe, our boy is in enemy territory ... I can't help being worried that he'll be captured and imprisoned, maybe shot."

"Jean, my love, you ought to know by now that Alec is a survivor. In a couple of months, he'll be right here, on leave ... have faith, lass."

"I dare say you're right, Joe. I'm glad you're here to get my head right and make me see sense."

"Oh, Jean, where else would I be?"

"It's been a while since Jim wrote to me ... I hope he's all right."

"Don't worry, Jean, he's not in France, he's just over the border in England."

Chapter 18

May, 1944

Alec is as high as a kite,
Inadvertently falling in love at first sight.

*A*lec finally pronounced himself fit enough to get back to England and, two days later, a Lysander arrived at the makeshift landing strip. Jeremy waved Alec goodbye, with instructions to tell Grace that he's looking forward to seeing her and holding wee Hope in his arms.

When Alec reported back at Tangmere, the CO immediately booked him into Chichester Hospital for a complete medical examination. As soon as that was completed, Alec was given two weeks leave while his results were being analysed.

When Alec sauntered into the family home in Bishopbriggs, his mother rushed to hug him. "Oh, Alec, you should have written or phoned to tell me you were coming. I'm shaking like a leaf ... you could have given me a heart attack."

"I'm sorry, Mum, everything's happened in a hurry ... but I thought it would be a pleasant surprise."

"Oh, it is, son ... my, you're looking well. How much leave do you have?"

"Two weeks, Mum, and I'm really pleased to be back home."

"I only wish you were home for good, Alec ... you haven't had much luck recently."

"You're wrong there, Mum. I've crashed two planes and I'm alive to tell the tale. I feel like the luckiest man in the RAF. Anyway, enough about me, is Grace around?"

"She's giving Kate a piano lesson ... come on through, they'll be pleased to see you."

"Hello, girls," said Alec, "don't let me interrupt the lesson."

"Oh, don't be daft, Alec," said Grace, "we have all the time in the world for that. It's great to see you, and looking so well. Well, come on, Alec, give us all your news."

"It just so happens, Grace, that I really have some news for you. I've spent some time with Jeremy ... he sends his love and looks forward to holding wee Hope in his arms."

Grace burst into tears but just as quickly smiled through the tears and said, "Where is he, Alec?"

"He's in northern France, where I was. He's with a French resistance group and he's safer there than he would be in London, getting bombed."

"I always told you, Jean, that he was alive", said Grace. "Now I understand why he hasn't been in contact."

"Yes, you did, lass, and I'm fair pleased that you've been proved right."

"I don't suppose he said when he will be coming home," said Grace.

"No, Grace, that would be out of his hands but, the way the war's going, I don't think it will be long till the Jerries are driven out of France."

Joe arrived and the family sat down to one of Jean's tasty spreads. "You look extraordinary healthy for a chap who's been recuperating from a crash in France," said Joe, "what's your secret, Alec?"

"I couldn't have been better looked after in the Glasgow Royal Infirmary, Joe. Actually, the bruises to my body took a couple of months to clear up. My secret is good luck. My navigator was killed outright in the crash landing ... he had no luck. Tomorrow, I've got to go and see his parents ... well, I don't **have** to do it but it seems the decent thing to do."

"Where do they live, Alec?"

"Springburn, Joe ... not far, but is there any chance of borrowing a car for the day?"

"Of course, ... I always have a spare one here. I'm pleased you're going to see your mate's folks, Alec. It'll mean a lot to them ... I'm real proud of you, son."

Alec parked the car on the street and looked at the old terrace house, a replica of every other dwelling on the short street. He lit a cigarette with difficulty, his hands shaking. Alec felt as nervous as he had been before the Amiens mission, wondering what kind of reception he would receive from Hec's parents. Ten minutes later, he finished his smoke, sighed, and walked quickly to the house.

Before he got a chance to knock, the door was opened by an attractive young brunette, smiling at his obvious discomfiture. "I've been watching you from the window for the last ten minutes. I thought you were never going to come in. I'm Sarah White."

Alec stared and stuttered, "I-I'm ..."

"Let me guess," said Sarah, "You are Alec MacDonald from Bishopbriggs. Come on through ... I'll put the kettle on. I'm Hector's sister, by the way."

"How did you know about me, Sarah?"

"Hector's last letter told us he'd been assigned to the crew of Squadron Leader Alec MacDonald, the best pilot in the squadron and a bit of a legend. He said you were practically a neighbour, coming from Bishopbriggs, so when I saw you in uniform, I put two and two together ... welcome to our house. My parents are both at work. Dad's a tram driver and Mum works in a munitions factory."

"I was hoping to see them, Sarah, to, you know ..."

"Yes, Alec, and they will appreciate a visit, rest assured about that. In the meantime, you're stuck with me. Unfortunately, I have to get back to Dunoon. I'm in the Wrens and my leave is up. Enjoy your cuppa while I get back into uniform."

Alec finished his tea as Sarah came back, looking even more attractive in her uniform. "When will your parents be home, Sarah?"

"I'm afraid it'll be a couple of hours, Alec ... I'm sorry, perhaps you can come back some evening."

"Let me drive you to the ferry, Sarah, then I'll see your parents on the way back."

"That would be great, Alec ... a chance to have a proper chat. OK, let's go."

Alec fully expected her to bombard him with questions about Hector's demise and was pleasantly surprised as she entertained him with light-hearted small talk. She had an infectious laugh and he felt himself warming to her vivacity.

"What do you do in the Wrens, Sarah?"

"Oh, I'm just a cook, Alec. I have no special skills ... I was a shop assistant before I was called up to beat Herr Hitler."

As she giggled at her quip, Alec laughed, responding in kind, "If Adolf knew you'd been called up, he'd be shaking in his shoes."

"I'll bet," laughed Sarah.

"Well, Sarah, here we are at the Broomielaw and the ferry awaits."

"Yes, I enjoyed our wee chat. Look, Alec, I don't want to know how my brother died but I have a favour to ask of you."

"Fire away, Sarah ... I'll do anything you want."

"When you're talking to my mum and dad, please, please tell them that Hector's death was instantaneous and painless. Do you mind doing that for me, Alec?"

"Sarah, that will be no problem as it is God's honest truth."

Sarah's eyes welled up and she brushed away the tears, "That's good, Alec ... I feel as if I can trust you. Well, that's that, thanks for the lift ... I suppose I'll never see you again."

"Never is a long time, Sarah. Would you mind if I write to you?"

She smiled as she got out of the car. "I'd like that, Alec. The address is HMS Osprey, Dunoon."

Alec watched admiringly as she boarded the ferry. When she reached the rails, she turned and waved to him. He returned her wave and headed back to Springburn, feeling an emotion he had never experienced before. He'd heard about it, he'd read about it, and he'd scoffed at it. Now, he was a believer in it ... love at first sight.

Next time Alec knocked, the door was opened by a man in a green tram driver's uniform. "Mr White, my name is Alec MacDonald ..."

"Come on in, son, I'm Tommy White, Hector's father. You're very welcome in this house."

"I'm on recuperation leave, Mr White ..."

"Oh, call me Tommy ... Louisa, we've got a visitor, young Alec MacDonald, come through and meet him."

Louisa came into the living room from the kitchen, drying her hands on a tea towel. "I'm pleased to meet you, Alec. Hector thought the world of you."

"It's lovely to meet you, Louisa," said Alec, "This is the first chance I've had to come here ... actually, that's not quite right, I met Sarah here earlier today and I drove her to the Dunoon ferry. She's a lovely girl ... you must be proud of her."

"Aye, she's a grand lass," said Tommy, "full of life."

"Ye'll stay for tea, Alec?" said Louisa. "I hope ye like tatties and mince."

"That's my favourite, Louisa ... I'll be delighted to stay."

Alec spent the following two hours in the company of two thoroughly decent ordinary Glaswegians, full of native humour, inquisitive about his family and what his plans were after the Nazis got their comeuppance. He told them he intended to write to Sarah and they seemed pleased to hear that. The dreaded question about Hector's death never arose, much to Alec's surprise and relief.

Finally, he rose to leave, and the couple hoped he'd come again, as often as he could. At the door, Tommy said, "We're really glad you survived that crash, Alec. You must have sustained some injuries yourself, though."

Louisa looked at him, silently pleading. Alec knew that this was the moment of truth. "Yes, I spent two months in France recuperating but

I was lucky ... Hector wasn't but, if it's any consolation, his death was instantaneous and painless."

"Oh, thank God, and thank you, Alec," said Louisa, tears streaming down her face. "Now, you've done your duty and Tommy and I appreciate that. Goodnight, son, and Godspeed."

Feeling happy and relieved as he drove back to Bishopbriggs, Alec was whistling a popular song of the day as he reached the family home.

Joe heard the off-key whistle, saw that the perpetrator was Alec and clapped both hands over his ears. Alec laughed, "Was it that bad, Joe?"

"Well, let me put it this way, son, I'm glad I didn't waste money getting you music lessons."

Alec was grinning from ear to ear, "Fair enough, Joe, you can't insult me today ... I feel on top of the world."

"OK, Alec, I can see you're dying to tell me some good news so, let's have it."

"Joe, you were spot on when you told me my navigator's folks would be pleased to see me. They couldn't have been nicer, gave me a nice meal, and asked me to come and see them whenever I had the chance."

"That's good, Alec, but hardly a reason for splitting my eardrums with your whistling. You're holding something back, aren't you, son?"

"You're spot on again, Joe ... you know more than your prayers. I hope I'm as wise as you when I get to your age."

"I'll ignore that insult. You're procrastinating, Alec, tell me the earth-shattering news."

"I've met the girl I'm going to marry, Joe. She's in the Wrens, stationed at Dunoon. I'm going to write to her, probably every day."

"Alec, wipe the stars from your eyes for a second ... where did you meet your intended?"

"Oh, didn't I tell you? She is Hec's sister, Sarah White. I met her before her parents came home. She is so vivacious ... I've never met anyone like her."

"That's great, son. Now if you'll calm down for a second, your young brother will be here tomorrow on a week's leave. I didn't expect that so soon so I'm not sure exactly what it means, Alec."

"I'd guess it's embarkation leave, Joe, but he wouldn't be allowed to divulge that. I reckon the allied forces will be invading Europe before long and of course, the medics will be needed."

"We'd better not tell your mother your suspicions, Alec ... it would worry her."

"Jim won't tell her either, Joe ... the powers that be wouldn't have told him ... that would be top-secret stuff, so mum's the word from you and me."

Chapter 19

Family reunion

Kate surprises as prodigy on the keyboard,
While wee Hope shows talent assembling a cheeseboard.

*J*im arrived on the following afternoon and there was a joyous reunion of the extended family. Joe sat at the head of the long table. "Well, here we are, happy to be together, three generations, from this old fellow right down to wee Hope, the bairn.

"Aye, we're blessed, Joe," said Jean, "it would be perfect if Jeremy were here with us."

"At least we know he's safe," said Grace. "It could be a lot worse ... I have a feeling that he'll be with us soon enough."

"I'm starving," said Hope, "I could eat a horse."

Everyone laughed and Jean and Grace got up to serve the piping-hot food.

"I've always been amazed, Jean, how you manage to serve such tasty food in these days of meat rationing," said Grace.

"Well, as you well know, we grow our own vegetables, Grace, plenty of them. A good cook can use them in different ways to make up for the scarcity of meat."

"She's a wonder woman in the kitchen," said Joe, "that's why I married her."

That remark produced much mirth, the adults well aware that, if ever a marriage was made in heaven, this was it.

"I have a piece of interesting family news," said Jean, smiling slyly.

"Well, Mum," said Jim, "are you going to share it or are we going to have to guess?"

"Your big brother is getting married."

Jim stared in astonishment at his brother, "Gee, Alec, that was quick."

"That's great, Alec," said Grace, "when's the big day?"

"Now, steady on, you lot," said Alec. "I only met the girl yesterday."

When the laughter subsided, Joe said, "Be that as it may, Alec, you told me you'd just met the girl you were going to marry."

"Yes, I did say that but ..."

"... but you haven't asked her yet," said Grace, "have you?"

"Well, no, but I did ask if I could write to her and she said she'd like that."

"Oh, now I get it," said Kate, "you're going to be pen pals."

"Yes, Kate, that's probably all we are at present," said Alec, "but I hope that something more will come of it later."

"Can you at least bring her home, Alec, so we can see her?" said Grace.

"Not for a while yet, Grace," said Alec, "she's in the Wrens and has just gone back after her leave. However, you can take my word for it that she is beautiful. Now, can we change the subject?"

"Oh, all right," said Grace, "I won't embarrass you anymore. What would you like to talk about?"

"How's my wee sister going with the piano?"

"Kate will be leaving school shortly. She doesn't want to go on to high school," said Grace, "but she, in my opinion, is good enough to win a scholarship to the Royal Scottish Academy of Music. Kate is a prodigy and her enthusiasm for a career as a classical pianist knows no bounds."

"Well," said Alec, "that's high praise indeed. Perhaps we can hear how much she has progressed. Would you favour us with a stave or two, Kate?"

"I'd love to, Alec, just as soon as wee Hope has finished stuffing her face with her second helping."

Everyone laughed and shortly repaired to the music room.

"What are you going to play, Kate?" asked Alec.

"Well, you may be disappointed, Alec," said Grace, "but it won't be the Beer Barrel Polka. Your wee sister will play Beethoven's Moonlight Sonata. Just sit back, close your eyes, and be enchanted."

As the last poignant notes lingered in the air, the silence was broken only by the slight sound of Joe, sobbing. He wiped his eyes and said, "That was beautiful, Kate."

"Thanks, Dad," said Kate, "I'm indebted to you for your encouragement."

Jim and Alec smiled at each other. They had long realised that Papa Joe Lennox was the only father Kate had known, so it came as no surprise to hear her calling Joe her Dad.

"I'm also grateful to Mum for getting Grace to tutor me," said Kate. "She is a wonderful teacher and a constant inspiration."

"And how about you, Hope," said Jean, "are you going to be a pianist too?"

"No fear, Nana, I'm going to be a cooker, just like you!"

Everyone laughed and Grace said, "I wouldn't be at all surprised. She's always helping her Nana in the kitchen."

While Kate continued to demonstrate her musical prowess, Alec drew Jim aside for a quiet word. "Mum is obviously delighted to accept wee Hope as her granddaughter ... that makes us uncles, Jim, doesn't it?"

"Yes, Alec, I don't mind at all ... we are part of a wonderful extended family, which includes Grace and Jeremy, headed by Papa Joe Lennox, but I reckon he'd be embarrassed if we started calling him Dad."

"You're right there, Jim," said Alec, "but he knows how highly we regard him. Let's leave it at that."

"Agreed, Joe knows more about human relations than we will ever know. Now, Alec, this girl they were teasing you about ... is she the real MacKay?"

"Brother, I've never been as certain of anything before. Now, I wouldn't blame you for doubting me ... after all, I've been too busy to get involved with girls in the past. Let's put it this way. The moment I clapped eyes on her, I was smitten. Later, as we talked, I was more than ever convinced that she is the one."

The leave went quickly by and Jean was tearful as she waved farewell to her two sons. Joe drove them to Central Station. "Well boys, let's hope we can all be together again soon. Good luck and God speed to you both."

Chapter 20

The two brothers, closer than ever before,
United by the advent of a horrible war.

When the boys had found a seat together in the packed train, Alec quietly asked, "Have you any idea why they gave you leave at this point, Jim?"

"I have a fair notion, Alec. They've been working us pretty hard on physical fitness, so I reckon there's a big job forthcoming."

"Overseas, Jim?"

"Yes, the scuttlebutt is that we're ready to invade Europe, so obviously casualties will be inevitable, hence the need for medicos."

"Joe and I guessed as much," said Alec. "I'm glad you didn't mention it to Mum."

"Well, despite the rumours among our mob, the operation and the date are bound to be top secret. I'll know soon enough, Alec. How about you, will you be flying again soon?"

"Oh, Jim. I've got a feeling in my water that they're gonna ground me. I've crashed two planes and been knocked about severely, including head injuries. They gave me leave while they analyse my medical examination results. I reckon they might think I'm jinxed."

"I know you've kept pretty quiet about your achievements," said Jim, "but I checked up on you a while back. It seems you are a bit of a legend in Fighter Command. You may have crashed two planes but you knocked at least five Jerries out of the air ... your record earned you a Distinguished Flying Cross, a DFC. The family knows nothing about that."

"Ah, Jim, if you can stay alive while mates are dying around you, gongs and promotion just happen. I'm no hero, I've just been bloody lucky. I never wanted to talk about it ... too much grief."

"Well, part of me wishes that you are grounded ... you've done enough, Alec, but I realise that a desk job may drive you crazy."

"You're right there, brother. I've been hoping that, if my tests results mean I can't fly, they might discharge me and I can resume my university degree course."

"Will you still study aeronautics, Alec?"

"No, as my piloting days will be over. I'll switch to mechanical engineering. There will be lots of opportunities in industrial Glasgow when I'm qualified."

"I must say that surprises me, Alec ... you have always been mad keen on aviation and the study of aeronautics."

"Jim, I'm gonna tell you something I never would have thought possible. I, too, hope they ground me permanently. I've seen too much death and destruction and for a while now I've been living a lie."

"In what way, Alec?"

"I filled a dead man's shoes to become Squadron Leader and I feel I've been living on borrowed time ever since. The God's honest truth is, now I'm shit-scared evert time I go into battle. I've survived on my natural flying skills but also because of good luck, which can't, on the law of averages, last much longer."

"Christ, Alec, can't you just tell your superiors that?"

"Oh, Jim, I've seen what happened to a young pilot when he refused to fly. His record was stamped with the dreaded judgement, lack of moral fibre ... a fancy way of branding him a coward."

"Did they court-martial him, Alec?"

"No, they showed some merciful understanding ... they put him in hospital for a rest, then organised a psychologist to talk to him, hopefully to effect a cure and get the youngster back in the air."

"Did it work, Alec?"

"I'm afraid not ... he was dishonourably discharged. I don't want to go through all that, Jim. I'd sooner take my chances in the air if they decree me fit enough to fly."

"I see ... thanks for confiding in me, Alec. We've never really been close, have we? You were the big brother, the tough rugby player, the warrior. I lived in your shadow, my only attribute being a talent for long-distance running, never a team hero. Now, it's my turn to tell **my** secret."

"Your secret? What secret could my wee brother possibly have to compare with what I've just told you?"

"Well, after you joined the RAF, I went through a dark period. Joe was aware of it but I couldn't tell him what my problem was. However, when Jeremy came to see me after he'd finished a Commando course in the Highlands, I opened up to him."

"Why Jeremy, Jim?"

"I'd always idolised him, Alec, and I felt that, if anyone could help me, it was him. So, I told him that I was opposed to killing another human being and, when called up for military service, I intended to register as a conscientious objector."

"Christ, Jim, how did he take that?"

"Very calmly ... he changed the subject, much to my surprise. He asked me what my career ambitions were. When I responded that I preferred to save lives by becoming a doctor, he smiled and offered me a solution which would prevent any embarrassment to myself or my family."

"And what was that, Jim?"

"He suggested that, as soon as I turned 18, I volunteer for the Royal Army Medical Corps. In the meantime, I should advise Joe of my desire to study medicine at the Uni, after I leave Allan Glen's School."

"And I assume you followed his advice?"

"Yes, but only after Joe overcame my worries about the cost involved. Jeremy said that life as a medico could be just as dangerous as that of a normal soldier but I assured him that was not a concern. I'd be happy to serve as a stretcher-bearer on the front line."

The train pulled into King's Cross station and the brothers stood on the platform. "Well, I guess this is where we part company," said Alec. "I'm heading for Chichester."

"And I'm going to Southampton," said Jim, "with the next stop France, shortly."

"Try not to worry, Jim ... Oh, Christ, what a piece of useless advice."

"I'm not worried, Alec ... there is a destiny that shapes our ends, rough-hew them as we may."

"What the hell's that, Jim?"

"Shakespeare, brother, Shakespeare," said Jim, laughing at Alec's confusion. "It means that if there's not a bullet with my name on it, I'll come home, safe and sound, OK?"

"Yeah, I suppose, but ..."

"But what?" said Jim.

"Oh, nothing," said Alec, as he hugged his brother. His voice broke as he said, "I just wish this fucking war was over."

Alec strode off hurriedly, not wanting Jim to see the tears streaming down his cheeks.

Chapter 21

Marching orders

The end of Alec's flying career is nearing,
Soon free to resume the course of engineering

Alec got off the train at Chichester and arrived at Tangmere airfield by taxi. He reported immediately to Wing Commander Hammond. "Ah, Mac, I trust you had a good leave."

"Yes, Sir, I did ... it was nice to catch up with my family. I also found time to pay my respects to Flight Sergeant White's parents. They live reasonably close to my folks."

"Really? That's useful ... I'll tell you why shortly but first I've got to deal with your medical report. I suppose you're anxious to hear it, Mac?"

"It **has** been on my mind, Sir."

"Sit down, Mac ... I was just going to have a drink. Would you join me in a drop of scotch?"

"I've never been much of a whisky drinker, Sir."

"Make an exception in this case, Mac ... humour me."

The CO poured two generous measures and handed one to Alec. "Cheers, Mac."

"Cheers, Sir," said Alec, sipping his drink, looking expectantly at his commanding officer.

"Well, Mac, I'm afraid you're not going to like my news. I won't beat about the bush ... your flying days are over. Now, I know your history ... you've virtually lived to be a pilot and I've never seen a better. However, the doctors tell us that your reflexes are not what they were ... one too many bangs on the head. Now, Mac, I don't have to tell you how long you'd last as a fighter pilot without fast reflexes."

"I see," said Mac, his facial expression inscrutable, hiding his relief. "What do I do now, Sir?"

"Well, son, you're still only 21, a full life ahead of you. After the experiences you've had, I don't imagine you'd be much use to us in a desk job, am I right?"

Grinning ruefully, Alec said, "That's true, Sir, but of course I'll do whatever I'm ordered."

"Well, I've consulted the area Group Captain, who is most reluctant to lose you to the RAF, so rather than grant you an honourable discharge, it has been agreed to keep you on the payroll, meagre though it is, but let you resume your university course. Group will require you to have a medical every 6 months, in the forlorn hope that your reflexes will have improved. So, Squadron Leader MacDonald, DFC, you have your orders. I trust, Mac, that this arrangement will atone for the loss of your flying career."

"What can I say, Sir? Under the circumstances, the RAF has been more than generous. Thank you, Sir."

"To sweeten the pot, you have been awarded a bar to your DFC for your part in Operation Jericho. For his contribution, Flight Sergeant Hector White has been posthumously awarded the DFM, Distinguished Flying Medal, and I'm hoping you will present it to his parents when you return to Glasgow."

"Nothing would give me greater pleasure, Sir."

On arrival in Glasgow in the evening, Alec's first port of call was the White residence in Springburn. He'd written to Sarah, giving her the news that his flying career was over but the RAF were holding on to him while he resumed his university course. He hoped to be able to visit her in Dunoon from time to time, as he was missing her terribly.

At Springburn, he was welcomed like a son and when he produced the medal, he could see the pride in their faces and the accompanying tears. "I'm back in Glasgow now, probably for the rest of the war," said Alec, "so I'll visit you as often as I can. At the weekend, I'm hoping to see Sarah in Dunoon."

"Oh, Alec," said Tommy, "You're out of luck there ... she is being posted to Belfast. She'll be in Ireland by the weekend. Here is her new address."

"Oh well, I'll have to content myself by writing to her often."

"If you like, Alec, come and see us on Saturday," said Louisa, "I'll make your favourite tatties and mince."

"OK, I'll look forward to that. Now, I'd better get going to Bishopbriggs. My folks are expecting me."

On Saturday, a distraught Tommy greeted Alec with the news that Louisa had been killed in a freak accident in the munitions factory where she worked. "Tommy," said Alec, "would you like to come home with me?"

"No son, at this time, I just want to grieve on my own. The funeral has been organised by her employer and will take place on Wednesday. I wrote to Sarah but I doubt if they'll grant her leave. Louisa is another casualty of war, like Hector."

"OK, Tommy, I'll see you on Wednesday."

When Alec returned home, he wrote a letter of condolence to Sarah, expressing heartfelt grief at the untimely death of her mother, a fine lady, the salt of the earth.

He assured Sarah that he would be at the funeral and would henceforth keep a regular check on her father.

Chapter 22

Although to peace he did aspire,
Jim experiences his baptism of fire.

*O*n D-Day, the 6th of June, Operation Overlord finally got underway. The long-promised invasion of Europe was a reality. 5000 vessels carrying around 3,000,000 troops set out to what was to be known as the Battle of Normandy.

Jim MacDonald found himself rubbing shoulders with troops in battledress, faces blackened, indistinguishable from one another. A medico friend, Harold Spencer, a Cambridge undergraduate, approached Jim and whispered, "I'm rather mystified, old boy ... I thought they were all British lads on board but I've just eavesdropped on a conversation among those four chaps over there by the rail. I speak a few languages but they have me beat. My best guess is they are Polish. Wander over, Jim, and have a listen."

Bewildered, but amused that his expert linguist friend was stumped, Jim was keen to hear this exotic tongue. Seconds after reaching the mysterious four, he retraced his steps, scarcely able to contain his mirth. Harold said, "You look mighty pleased with yourself, Jim ... I didn't know you spoke other languages. Come on then, enlighten me."

"Don't feel too bad, Harold ... those are four Scottish guys talking Glaswegian, the street dialect of my own youth."

"My God, they look so serious ... what were they talking about, Jim, the forthcoming battle?"

"No, Harold, something much more serious ... their religion, that's Scottish football, Rangers and Celtic."

As the flotilla approached the French coast, the small talk ceased as the troops prepared to disembark in the shallows. Wave after wave of soldiers swarmed on to the beach, hurrying to attain cover from the German machine guns on the cliff tops.

The medicos followed, attending to the many casualties who had borne the brunt of the enemy bombardment.

Jim was appalled by the extent of the carnage. He, along with the many other Medical Corps personnel were flat out, sorting out the dead and giving morphine to the wounded. Ultimately, the German machine guns were silenced and the British troops were over the cliffs and pushing the enemy southwards.

After the medics stretchered the badly wounded back to the ships, they were ordered to catch up with the invasion forces, who doubtless were sustaining more casualties as they pushed inland.

The advance continued and spread out over a wide front. Jim and Harold were attached to a company of the Highland Light Infantry, which carefully made its way through forest country. Emerging into open territory, the troops were confronted by a steep hill, at the top of which was a machine gun nest which opened fire and mowed down a dozen soldiers. The rest of the company retreated to the shelter of the forest. Captain Jarvie consulted his right-hand man, Sergeant Macmillan. "We've got to find a way to stop that bastard, Sarge. We're stuck here until we can take him out ... any ideas?"

"There's some low cover on the left, Sir. I reckon a few of us on our bellies might be able to get up just below the ridge he's on. I'll take Macfarlane and Smith and try to get close enough to lob a couple of grenades over the ridge."

As the three men set off, Captain Jarvie called up Jim and Harold. "Can you guys follow those men at a safe distance, just in case. Crawl like them and for Christ's sake keep your heads down, OK?"

"No problem, Sir, we're a couple of skinny buggers," said Jim. "No one will spot us in the long grass over there."

Obeying instructions to the letter, the medics stayed 20 yards behind the soldiers. Progress was inevitably slow, inching along on their stomachs. A sudden burst of machine gun fire resulted in Macfarlane and Smith being hit. As Jim reached them, he quickly determined they were both beyond help. He took their hand grenades and signalled to Harold that they carry on behind the sergeant. Jim thought, "He's nearly reached the ridge ... he's going to make it."

Seconds later, he heard a stifled yelp of pain as the sergeant disappeared from view. He crawled as fast as he could to find out what had happened to the sergeant. There had been no gunfire ... what the hell was going on?

Meanwhile, Harold had been struggling to keep up. The effort proved fatal as, in his haste, he exposed enough of his body for the machine gunner to riddle him with bullets. Jim crawled back to confirm the heartbreaking fact that his best mate had breathed his last. He experienced an anger, foreign to his nature, determined to help the sergeant kill the German bastard who'd murdered his friend.

Continuing up the hill, Jim reached a shell crater into which the sergeant had fallen. "Where's it hurting, Sarge?"

"My shoulder, mate ... I'm in fuckin' agony. Look, just gimme a painkiller so that I can do what we came up here to do."

"Sarge, you have a fractured clavicle ... you're going nowhere."

"Listen, sonny, that Jerry has got to be taken out ... do as I ask, for Christ's sake."

"I'll fix him," said Jim, "I've got your mates' grenades ... I'll take yours as well."

"You're a medic, son, this isn't your caper ... why are you risking your life?"

"If I don't do this, my friend's life will have been in vain, as well as your boys."

"What's your name, son?"

"Jim MacDonald ... listen, Sarge, if I don't make it, promise me you'll let my folks know."

"OK, Jim, just move slowly and quietly along the ridge and lob all those grenades. Take that fucker out. Good luck!"

Contrary to the sergeant's instructions, Jim threw caution to the winds, running quickly to the middle of the ridge, lobbing all the grenades as fast as he could. He then clambered over the top of the ridge, verifying that the gunner had been silenced. He turned, facing down the hill and waved his arms triumphantly, aware that Captain Jarvie would be watching impatiently for such a signal.

The troops quickly emerged from the forest and came up the hill. Captain Jarvie said to Jim, "Where's Sergeant Macmillan and the others, Private?"

"The sergeant is in that crater over there. He has a fractured clavicle. He's in a deal of pain ... I gave him morphine, so he'll be very groggy now. The others are dead, including my medic partner."

"Well, thanks to you, Private, we can get on with it, but you took a helluva risk, careering across the ridge like that. What on earth were you thinking?"

"I just saw red, Sir, and wanted to avenge my mate as quickly as possible."

"Well, son, if you keep on seeing red, you'll end up bloody dead, but well done. Now, let's get to my sergeant."

The sergeant was incoherent, almost asleep in the crater. "You stay with him, Private ... the rest of the battalion are right behind us. The medics with them will help you, OK?"

"Yes, Sir ... I reckon I gave the Sarge a wee bit too much morphine, but he **was** in agony."

"What's your name, Private?"

"Jim MacDonald, Sir."

"I'm sorry about your mate, son. Have a wee rest alongside Sergeant Macmillan and let that adrenaline subside."

Chapter 23

July, 1944

Jim's military exploits reduced to zero,
Hospitalised now, a reluctant hero.

As the Allies advanced deeper into enemy-held territory, they met stubborn resistance and suffered many more casualties. The medics were kept busy to the point of exhaustion and, on the fourth of July, normally a cause for celebration for the Yanks, Private Jim MacDonald, RAMC, collapsed, ostensibly from fatigue but later diagnosed as pleurisy.

Jim was flown to London and placed in the care of Guy's Hospital. Further tests led to the conclusion that he had developed pleural tuberculosis. It was decided that he be transferred to a military-run sanatorium in the Scottish Highlands, where clean fresh air would be beneficial. He was still a Private in the Royal Army Medical Corps, although it appeared likely that he would ultimately be discharged on medical grounds.

On July 31, he received a surprise visit from a Colonel of the Highland Light Infantry.

"Private MacDonald, you have been mentioned in dispatches by Captain Jarvie, for courage shown in battle, well beyond the call of duty. Consequently, I have great pleasure in telling you that you have been awarded the Military Medal."

"Thank you, Sir ... this comes as a complete surprise. I really don't feel I deserve the honour."

"Two reliable eyewitnesses, Captain Jarvie and Sergeant Macmillan, place your action in the top rank. Surely you won't dispute the word of those experienced soldiers?"

"Oh no, Sir ... it's just that I was the last man standing ... I **had** to do it."

"Whatever your reasoning, Private, your action saved the lives of more HLI soldiers. Accept the medal and wear it with pride."

Chapter 24

Jeremy's undercover work now complete,
His boss in London he must meet.

When the Allied army freed Amiens, Henri Montand and his resistance group were welcomed by the invasion force as a Free French special operations group and surged south, keen to rid their beloved France of the hated Boches.

Mike Ferguson expected to be ordered to resume regular soldiering but was pleasantly surprised when the Foreign Office decided to leave him in Amiens as a 'sleeper', for the time being, to maintain a watching and listening brief. It was thought likely that there were Vichy French Nazi sympathisers in the town and perhaps German agents. Yvette was delighted, having expected to be parted from her live-in lover for the duration of the war.

Jeremy contacted Colonel Nicholson as soon as Amiens had been liberated, expecting to be ordered to join the invasion force. "Henri Montand and his resistance group are now part of General de Gaulle's Free French army, Colonel. Do you want me to follow on, as liaison, or ...?"

"Negative, Jeremy," interrupted the Colonel, "your job there is over. Tomorrow morning, a Lysander will pick you up and bring you to London. Report to me when you arrive."

Chapter 25

Respite from clear and present danger

Wee Hope finally meets her father,
Who belatedly weds her happy mother.

"Welcome back to this tight little isle, Jeremy," said Colonel Nicholson, "I must say you're looking well after your sojourn in France. Tell me, have you kept up your physical fitness?"

"Colonel, if I hadn't, I'd probably have met my maker in all the sorties with those French Resistance guys."

"Good man ... do you remember Lt Col Wallace, the Commando trainer at Achnacarry?"

"How could I forget him, Sir? ... Willie Wallace, the slave master. I called him Braveheart."

"Well, he hasn't forgotten you either. He keeps ringing me to see if you're available, Jeremy."

"Available for what, Sir?"

"He's snowed under, Jeremy, with an increased demand for Commandos. As you're no doubt aware, they are in a high-risk occupation ... the turnover of those lads is considerable. He needs a right-hand man who is tough and capable to share the load. He needs to split the lads into two manageable groups, one of which to be headed by you. You really made a great impression on Wallace, Jeremy."

"Well, Sir, I suppose I should be flattered but is this what you want me to do?"

"It does come under my umbrella of Strategic Services, Jeremy. Now, with the allied invasion of Europe well under way, I can't think of a more important task and you are the man to fill it. I've informed your Braveheart that you will report to him mid-August. Until then, you have earned some leave. From what Squadron Leader Alec MacDonald told me, you'll be keen to see your fiancée and your young daughter.

So, Jeremy, use my phone ... ring your girl and tell her you're on the way. I'll be in touch from time to time."

Grace Devine drove to Glasgow Central station to meet Jem as he alighted from the overnight train from London. He held her in close embrace until she gasped, "I can't breathe, Jem."

He held her at arms-length. "I'm sorry, darling, let me have a look at you ... my God, you are more beautiful than ever. I know we agreed not to marry while the war was on but wee Hope has changed that, hasn't she? Will you marry me now, my love?"

"Oh, Jem, I'm glad you have proposed because I've already organised a civil ceremony for tomorrow. So, sweetheart, I accept with all my heart, even though it sounds a bit like a shotgun wedding."

Jem laughed, "Hope is 4yo, Grace ... it's a greatly delayed shotgun wedding. Well done, my darling ... have I told you lately that I love you?"

"Not lately, Jem, but we'll catch up, I'm sure. Jean has organised a double bed in my room so she and Joe regard our marriage as a fait accompli."

"I can't wait to see Hope ... have you told her who I am?"

"Yes, Daddy ... Joe is Gramps, Jean is Nana, Kate is Auntie, and Alec and Jim are her uncles. She is the baby of a large family and will have no trouble in accepting you. Darling, wee Hope is quite a character ... you may be in for a big surprise."

"Grace, I'm getting used to surprises ... another one won't shock me."

"Right, here's the car ... you can drive. Your extended family awaits your arrival ... I reckon Jean has killed the fatted calf to welcome back the prodigal son."

Jean embraced Jeremy, "Welcome home, son. Now, the others can wait ... you only have eyes for Hope. Say hello to your daddy, Hope."

Hope regarded him quizzically, "Hello, Daddy, where have you been hiding?"

Jeremy swept her up into his arms, "I've been hiding in France, in the army, just like a lot of other daddies."

"Can you show me your medals?"

"Oh, sweetheart, I don't have any medals to show you. You have to do very brave things to get medals ... are you disappointed?"

"Not really, but Uncle Alec has two medals. Was he braver than you?"

"Your uncle Alec was very brave ... not everyone can be as brave as him, Hope."

"Your Daddy was very brave, Hope", said Grace, "but nobody knows about it yet. Someday, he'll be able to show you a medal or two."

"Oh, that's OK, I love Uncle Jim, and he doesn't have any medals either."

Jeremy and Grace were wed at Glasgow Registry Office and set off immediately on a weekend honeymoon. They drove though the beautiful Trossachs until they reached Callander. To their surprise, the manager of the Callander Hotel of four years previous was still in charge. Recognising

Grace, he asked if he would be out of order in asking her to play piano for the diners.

"You'll have to ask Major Cowan, my husband."

"I'd like nothing better," said Jeremy.

At the end of the evening, the couple made glorious love, with no thought of rhythm method or any other form of contraception.

"You realise, Jem, that I shall in all probability get pregnant."

"No doubt, my darling," said Jeremy, "and no doubt you've already selected a name."

"Yes, Daddy, if we have another girl, I'd like to name her Faith. However, if we have a boy, I want you to name him."

"Fair enough, Grace ... I don't even have to think about it. He shall be called Joseph, in honour of the finest man I've ever known."

"Joe Cowan," mused Grace, "of course, named after Joe Lennox, who else? ... I like it."

"Well, now that's settled, let's get back to wee Hope, our eternal bond. I'd like to spend as much time with her as possible. Four years of catch-up won't be easy, Grace. After all, I'm a complete stranger to the wee lassie."

"Oh, come on, Jem, you could charm the hind legs off a donkey," laughed Grace. "You charmed me pretty quickly ... soon, your daughter will be eating out of your hand."

"I'm not sure about your mixed metaphors but I assume you are being complimentary. Grace, I can detect the influence of your Irish mother and I'm sure that contributes to **your** charm".

Grace was right ... wee Hope quickly accepted Jeremy as her father. Of course, she trusted her mother and her nana, believing everything they said. As they constantly sang the praises of Jeremy, it was not surprising that she paid close attention to him and soon fell under his spell.

"Now that you've won your daughter's heart, Jem," said Grace, "why don't you and Alec pay a visit to Jim? As you are both in uniform, you'll have no trouble gaining access to the military hospital. The family can get along without the pair of you for a day or two."

So, Squadron Leader MacDonald and Major Cowan drove to the Grampians in the Highlands. "You realise, Jeremy, that Jim has tuberculosis. We may not be able to get close to him."

"Oh well, we'll still be able to communicate and find out how he's getting on. Jesus, Alec, it's still summer but it would freeze the medals off a brass general up here."

"Yes, but take in a lungful of the cold fresh air … it's nectar. That's why they have sanatoriums up here, Jeremy."

Alec parked the car and they made their way to Reception. "We'd like to see Private James MacDonald, if that's possible," said Alec.

"Are you family members, gentlemen?"

"Yes, I'm his brother and Major Cowan is a brother-in-law."

"Fine … well you've arrived at an opportune moment because he has just been declared non-infectious. If you walk through that side door, you'll find him in the garden."

"There he is," said Alec, "in full uniform, chatting up a pretty girl."

"Yes, she's a looker all right and he looks well too," said Jeremy, "that cold fresh air must be agreeing with him."

The girl left before Jim saw his brother and Jeremy approach.

"Jimmy boy, you're looking really well. Is that because of your beautiful girl friend who's just left?"

"Alec, behave yourself, she's not my girlfriend, she's a student nurse, OK? Now, how are you, Jeremy?"

"I've never been better, Jim, although just a wee bit perplexed. If I'm not mistaken, your uniform ribbon shows you've won the Military Medal. That's a wee bit unusual for a private in the Medical Corps."

"Oh, it's a long story. I just found myself in a certain situation. The reality is that my experience in France has convinced me that that you were right. That bastard, Hitler, has to be stopped."

"I assume then," said Alec, "that you are no longer a pacifist."

"Jim, what's happening with your illness?" interrupted Jeremy, "You look really well. Now tell us, what's going on?"

"Well, boys, appearances can be deceptive. They may have to do some exploratory surgery to see the condition of my left lung. However, they'll wait to see if this pure fresh air works its wonders."

"How do they check your progress. Jim?" asked Jeremy.

"Well, that young nurse subjects me to a stress test every week. While I'm puffing, she measures my pulse rate, blood pressure, temperature, keeping a chart on my progress."

"How long do you reckon all that's gonna take, Jim?"

"How long's a piece of string, Alec? It could take a year. Anyway, it's not all bad, the nurse pops in to see me every day."

"I knew it," said Alec, "she **is** your girlfriend."

Jim laughed, "No, brother, she's not, but there **is** a loose connection to our family. That's why she makes a point of coming to see me daily. Her mother insists on it."

"Jesus, Jim," said Alec, "Now I'm more confused than ever. What's her mother got to do with it?"

"Her mother was matron of honour at our mum's wedding to Joe. They have kept in touch and been friends ever since. Her father was best man."

"Have these mystery people got a name, Jim?" asked Jeremy.

"Yes, Angus and Kirsty Stewart," said Jim, "and they live in Inverness."

"I'm beginning to see the light," said Jeremy. "Angus Stewart is in charge of all Co-op operations in the Highlands. He answers directly to Joe Lennox."

"Well, Jim," said Alec, "you and I were at the wedding but I don't remember them, do you?"

"Not really," said Jim, "but we were very young kids then. Anyway, Fiona Stewart, my nurse, is their 18yo daughter. She would only have been four then. We never met her ... her grandmother looked after her a lot at the time as Kirsty was a busy GP in Inverness. Now, it appears that Kirsty has been writing to our mum, keeping her up to date on my health."

"Still," leered Alec, "be that as it may, brother, I can tell that you are attracted to your nurse."

"Naturally, I am, brother, I'm not a kid any longer and ... well you've had an eyeful of her. Can you blame me?"

"Not in the slightest, Jim," said Alec, "have you told her of your feelings?"

"How can I, Alec? I have TB, it wouldn't be fair to put her in such a position. No, brother, I must await the final outcome of my condition. Jeremy, you must see that I'm doing the right thing, don't you?"

"Jim, I wouldn't expect any less of you," said Jeremy. "Give it time, enjoy your friendship with young Fiona. After all, you are both very young, despite wartime experiences. Be patient, Jim, I have a feeling that something good will come of this."

"Me too," said Alec. "Now, we are getting the message that our time here is up. Let's go, Jeremy."

As they drove away, Jeremy said, "I've just realised that Achnacarry, my next posting, is only a short drive from the sanatorium. I'll be able to visit Jim regularly."

"I hope the poor bugger isn't gonna be there for a year," said Alec, "even if he has the luxury of being looked after by that gorgeous piece of crackling. On the other hand, if he gets the all-clear quickly, I hate the thought of him being sent back into action, especially as you and I have been spared that."

"I understand what you're saying, Alec. You love your young brother, don't you, although you were the tough guy who would never have admitted that? Now, he's turned out to be a hero, surprisingly, and you hate the thought of losing him."

"Jeremy, you are a pretty smart bastard. Now I can understand why my young brother confided in you. Look, Jeremy, I'm the rough, tough air ace who ought to have been killed many times. I survived through sheer luck. I hate the idea of young Jim in action again. He may not be so lucky."

"Alec, Alec, there's a war on ... we can't control any of that. You'll just have to let it be. If Jim has to go back, my guess is that the MacDonald luck will continue."

"Well, Jeremy, you've been right about everything else. I just hope you're right about that."

"Oh, Alec, I'm no guru. I just wish this bloody war would come to a speedy end."

Jeremy took up his posting at Achnacarry and, at the first opportunity, popped into the sanatorium to see Jim. "How's tricks, Jim?"

"Oh, Jeremy, I can't complain but I get a mite frustrated ... it's taking too long."

"Last time I was here, you seemed happy enough, with the young nurse seeing you every day. Have you grown tired of her attention, Jim?"

"On the contrary, I've fallen for her but, as I explained, I'm not in a position to tell her of my feelings. In fact, I'm trying to be aloof and I hate myself for that. That's one reason for my frustration, Jeremy."

"Oh, Jimmy boy, aloof is not good ... it sounds rude and that's not your nature. Can't you just be friendly and be patient? There's something you're not telling me. Come on, tell me what's going on."

"Christ, Jeremy, you've always been able to read my mind. OK, well, I can't be sure but I think she has feelings for me beyond the nurse/patient relationship."

"Can you hear yourself, Jim?" said Jeremy, unable to stop laughing. "Most blokes would bend over backwards to win the heart of the fair damsel, yet, here you are, fighting off the lass you profess to love, although she seems to be willing."

"Damn it, it's not funny, Jeremy. You're not being much help."

"No, I'm not ... do you want my advice?"

"Well, that depends ... what do you suggest?"

"Your ethics are to be admired, Jim, but you may be too goody-goody. Cut this aloof crap and return the girl's friendliness. If, as you suspect, the love is mutual, sooner or later, it will come out in the open. My advice is to let the chips fall where they may and deal then with any problems arising."

On his next visit, Jeremy found Jim asleep in a chair in the garden. The nurse was present and Jeremy introduced himself. "Hi, I'm Jeremy Cowan, a personal friend of Jim."

"Yes, I've heard of you, although we've never crossed paths. I'm Fiona Stewart."

"I know your father, Fiona. Before the war, I worked for Joe Lennox, as a lawyer for the Co-op. I met your father when Joe appointed him manager of the Inverness branch. Now, enlighten me, Fiona, why is Jim asleep at eleven o'clock in the morning?"

Fiona smiled, "I put him through his weekly stress test earlier, Jeremy. It's not unusual for him to have a nap afterwards."

"I see, ... how is he progressing, Fiona? I know he's been a bit down recently."

"Health-wise, he's improving slowly, but there was a spell when he seemed depressed. I made a point of seeing him every day but his body language was telling me that he preferred to be alone."

"That surprises me," said Jeremy, "I suppose you had to back off?"

"I did, but he suddenly snapped out of that and told me that he looks forward to my daily visits."

Jeremy suppressed a smile, in the realisation that Jim had acted on his advice.

"Fiona, I have the feeling that you are giving Jim special treatment, above and beyond the call of duty, as it were. Am I right?"

"Oh, God, is it that obvious? You know, Jeremy, when I began nursing, I was told it was not a good idea to become personally involved with patients because they either die or leave and you get hurt. However, Jim is special ... he is really a bit of a loner, and yet his wardmates think the world of him."

"Is it because he's a bit of a hero?" said Jeremy, "medal winner and all that?"

"No, no, they wouldn't know about that. A couple of them seek help with letters they write home. They can tell he's an educated man and, as they have spelling difficulties, he virtually writes for them. He never rejects them, although it consumes a lot of his time every week."

"Well, I don't suppose he has much else to occupy his mind, Fiona."

"Actually, Jeremy, you couldn't be more wrong. Jim spends most of his time writing in a scrap pad he asked me for. This morning, as I approached him for his stress test, he was head down, concentrating on his writing. When I asked him what he was doing, he replied that it was just some scribbling. He tore it off the pad, crunched it up and threw it in the waste paper bin. I've just retrieved it and I'd like you to read it out loud, to me."

"OK," said Jeremy, "here goes;"

> *As the sun-filled days are drawing in,*
> *The humming of the bees is stilled,*
> *while the russet leaves are falling fast,*
> *The poet reaches for his Autumn quill.*

"Well, Jeremy, isn't it obvious that Jim is a natural poet?"

"I've always been aware of Jim's love of poetry and literature," said Jeremy. "He could quote Shakespeare and make it apply it to the situation of the day. Writing was his first love but he realised that he couldn't earn a living at it. He chose medicine and had done around a year at uni prior to volunteering for The Royal Army Medical Corps. I expect he's just passing time, writing bits and pieces to keep his brain occupied."

"I expect you're right, Jeremy, but he **is** talented. He has become very special to me and I look forward to talking to him every day ... yes, defying the advice from my superiors."

"Well, Fiona, I've enjoyed our wee chat. I won't hang around for him to wake up. Next time I'll come on a day when he hasn't had his stress test."

Six days later, Jeremy saw Fiona in Reception before visiting Jim. "Ah, Jeremy, I'm glad I've bumped into you. I've got hold of another of Jim's scribbles. I'd like you to read it to me, please."

He saw that Jim had entitled a poem, Lament for the Sojer Laddies. He began to read;

> *When economic gloom pervades the land*
> *And children go to bed with hunger pang,*
> *Too soon we'll hear the patriotic band*
> *Exhorting us to go to war again.*
>
> *The moneymen at work behind the scene*
> *Control us all like puppets on a string.*
> *The gnomes of Zurich recognise no king or queen*
> *And national borders do not mean a thing.*

Your country needs you! Do not let it down.
The young heroic lads will heed the cry,
Mere cannon fodder, scattered on the ground,
Like flowers left to wither, and then die.

The tunes of glory fade amid the gore,
Until next time ... the tragedy of war.

As Jeremy finished, he looked up to see Fiona weeping. "It **is** an emotional piece, lass," he said.

"Oh God, Jeremy, he's pouring his heart out there," stammered Fiona, "but don't you think it is also brilliant?"

"It's a classic sonnet, no doubt about that, lassie. I'll go and see him now, and maybe find out what's going through his head."

"I hope you'll encourage him to continue his writing, Jeremy. I'm sure that even you can now see that Jim is something special."

❧

"Ah, Jeremy, the very man I wanted to see," said Jim.

"Well, here I am, Jim ... what's on your mind?"

"I've decided not to pursue a medical career. You gave me good advice, for which I'll be eternally grateful, but I've seen enough blood and slaughter to last me for a lifetime. I wouldn't have the stomach for surgery now."

"I can understand that, Jim, but what do you have in mind now?"

"I've a notion to follow in your footsteps and study law."

"That could be great, Jim. We may even become partners, brothers-in-law, as it were," quipped Jeremy. "I'll give you all the help I can. Now, how are things on the health front? Is your young nurse pleased with your progress?"

"Fine, Jeremy, improving every week, although too slowly for my liking. Still, I've listened to your sage advice and am enjoying her company every day, while reluctantly struggling to keep my hands off her."

"Good, Jim ... I hear you're doing a bit of writing to pass the time ... anything interesting?"

131

"Oh, ideas come to me and I've taken to scribbling them down, perhaps to refine them later, in verse form. I've always liked poetry, as you are well aware. As you said, it's my way of passing time until I get my final health report, good or bad."

"Well, I reckon that's a great idea, Jim. I'd like to read some of your verses, when you are happy with them. I'm not a literary Philistine, despite being a staid and sober lawyer."

Chapter 26

Good times ahead

Jem and Grace have a baby boy
While Jim has tidings of great joy.

*O*n April 13th, 1945, Grace Cowan gave birth to a healthy baby boy. By this time, Jeremy was known to all and sundry as Jem, due no doubt to Grace's influence.

Jem told Joe that he intended to name the baby Joseph but, to his surprise, Joe said, "I appreciate the thought, Jem, but I've always hated my name. If you don't mind, can I suggest something more regal?"

"Of course, Joe, what do you have in mind?"

"Malcolm, a Scottish kingly name, as befits a son of Jem and Grace, two people of real royalty whom I've grown to love and respect. If you feel that you must include me, name the wee fellow Malcolm Joseph Cowan."

Grace applauded the decision and added that she wanted her baby baptised in Jean's Presbyterian church. As Grace and Jem were not particularly religious, they were happy to honour Jean in this way, confirming that their extended family would never suffer religious contention.

Three months later, Jim received the welcome news that his left lung had responded favourably to the pure fresh Highland air. His stress tests were no longer stressful and there was no need for exploratory surgery. He was declared 100% fit for active duty. He thanked Fiona for her help in his treatment and promised to write to her regularly.

However, the powers that be decided that he would be more useful as a nursing aide in the sanitorium as they were suffering staff shortages. The war was going well for the allies and a German surrender was deemed imminent.

On hearing this from a compassionate RAMC colonel, Jim, now out of danger, felt free to unburden his soul. "Fiona, as I've now been cleared of TB and not going back overseas, I can now confess that I've been in love with you for ages."

"Oh, Jim, I thought you were going to disappear without ever telling me. For my part, I had feelings for you from the first day you were assigned to my care. Those feelings soon developed into true love, darling."

"Really, Fiona? Why didn't you tell me?"

"I was waiting for you, Jim. The man should always make the first move."

"Well, in that case, will you marry me, Fiona?"

"Yes, yes, yes, and the sooner the better."

"Well, now that I'm no longer confined to barracks, I want to visit your parents and ask your dad for your hand in marriage."

"Oh, honey, that's so old-fashioned ... this is 1945."

"Nevertheless, your folks may have some reservations about my health, Fiona. I just want to be sure, OK?"

On the following weekend, Jim confronted Angus and Kirsty Stewart. "I want to marry your daughter. I've just turned twenty-one years of age, a private in the Royal Army Medical Corps, with no personal fortune and, as yet, no means of earning a living after the war."

Angus and Kirsty looked at each other and nodded. "I think I can speak for my wife, Jim. We would welcome you into our family wholeheartedly. A son of Jean Lennox would be the finest bloodlines we could wish for Fiona."

"That's a lovely compliment," said an embarrassed Jim, "especially as I can't even afford to buy an engagement ring."

Kirsty laughed, "Don't worry about that, Jim. She can have my mum's engagement ring. Here it is, Jim ... present it to Fiona. There's a war on, you know ... money is as scarce as hen's teeth."

Jim spluttered, "Oh, Mrs Stewart, I reckon you're going to be the best mother-in-law I'll ever have!"

"Well, thanks for that," laughed Kirsty, "but I hope I'll be the only mother-in-law you'll ever have."

Angus intervened to spare the young man further embarrassment. "This war will be over soon, Jim. I suggest that you delay any wedding plans until the inevitable celebrations are over."

"My sentiments exactly, Mr Stewart," agreed Jim, "and that'll give me time to buy a wedding ring."

"Fine, son ... well, you've done your duty," said Angus, "now, it's time for you to get back to work. Go, Jim, and rest assured, it is with our blessing."

As predicted, the war ended in September and the war-weary British civilians celebrated with bonfires and dancing in the streets all over the country. The impromptu parties continued for the best part of a week, after which it was obvious that the massive post-war rebuilding of the economy had to be undertaken quickly. The country was bankrupt and had to borrow under the Marshall Plan. The demise of the British Empire was imminent but the ordinary citizens couldn't have cared less. They had suffered so much and now just wanted to have a job and live without the nightly fear of being bombed out.

Chapter 27

Alec gets demobilised

Sarah won't countenance further delay,
So, she and Alec wed straightaway.

*A*lec informed his superior officer that he no longer wanted a career in the Royal Air Force and was demobilised forthwith. As his university course had been won on a scholarship, his honesty to the RAF only deprived him of the wage, however meagre, of a Squadron Leader.

Joe Lennox, true to form, was happy to support a beloved family member and a war hero to boot, so that Alec could complete his university degree.

Alec had been visiting Sarah's dad at least once per week and writing regularly to Sarah, who had been transferred from Dunoon to Belfast for the duration of the war.

Now, Sarah was home, also demobilised, and Alec's sole remaining problem was how he could propose to Sarah White without the glamorous Squadron Leader's uniform, uncertain of her reply, particularly as he was honour-bound to confess that it could be 3 years before he could support her.

He had been writing to her regularly, confessing his love, but as she had spent the rest of the war in Belfast, he hadn't met her face to face since that first dramatic occasion, and he was naturally worried.

Now, as he reached her Springburn address, he reached for a cigarette to steady his nerves but quickly realised he'd given up the smokes a couple of years earlier. Now, he was on his own ... some hero, scared to confront a wee lassie.

He knocked on the door, which was immediate opened by Sarah, in a smart 2-piece suit, and still radiantly beautiful. He was transfixed, struggling to speak.

"Oh God, Alec, as I recall, you were tongue-tied when we first met and it's happening again. I fondly imagined that you would tell me you loved me and take me in your arms. Now, it seems that I have to take the initiative. Come on, darling, kiss me. I've thought of nothing else since I received your first letter."

Alec caressed her, kissing her passionately, whispering his undying love.

"I want you to be my wife, Sarah but, at the moment, I can't give you the life you deserve. Can you wait 3 years, darling?"

"I could, but I don't intend to. I want you now, Alec. I'm from the Glasgow working class ... we'll make do, darling, marry me now! Christ, haven't we waited long enough?"

"But, Sarah, let's be practical ... I haven't got a job. It'll be 3 years before I'm qualified in engineering and we haven't got a place to live yet."

"Minor details, Alec. I've found a job already ... canteen cook at North British Locomotive Works, right here in Springburn. We could live here. Now I'm home, I'll be looking after Dad. So, if you're agreeable, I can look after you too. Actually, North British are looking for budding engineers. I have an uncle who is a draughtsman there ... they have some sort of scheme starting up for returned servicemen. Why don't you have a wee informal chat to him, Alec? Look, we'll postpone the wedding until you've had a chance to clear your mind, OK?"

"Jesus, Sarah, you've taken the wind out of my sails."

"Darling, you didn't have any wind in your sails. Now, drive me to my new job and I'll introduce you to Grant Blair, my uncle."

"OK, OK, God, you don't waste any time, do you?"

"Alec, haven't we wasted enough time already? Let's do this."

"Uncle Grant, meet Alec MacDonald, my husband-to-be. He's 23, ex-Squadron Leader fighter pilot, with one and a half years studying engineering at university. I'll leave him with you."

Grant grinned and shook hands. "That Sarah doesn't muck around, does she, Alec?"

"She's a live-wire alright. Look Grant, I really don't know why I'm here. She railroaded me into coming ... said you may have some suggestions for me."

"I see ... well, tell me what you had in mind, Alec, before today."

"Well, another two and a half years at uni, get a degree, then a job. That was the plan. I asked Sarah to wait 3 years to get married but she won't have a bar of that."

"OK," said Grant, "it's been our experience that uni graduates are virtually useless to us until they get their hands dirty learning the practical side of the business. That could take quite a while before they start to earn their keep."

"Yes, I can understand that. I'd be in that category. The only job I've had is flying, but Sarah said that you have some sort of scheme for blokes like me."

"Yes, that's true ... we call it a sandwich scheme and it's designed specifically for ex-servicemen like yourself. It's really an adult apprenticeship in which we fast-track you through the toolroom, learning the use of hand tools, then all the different machine tools, like the lathe, milling machine, grinder, etc. From there you go to the drawing office, learning technical drawing and draughtsmanship.

All that occupies 4 days of the working week. The 5th day, we send you to the Royal Technical College for engineering theory. Also, you'd be expected to attend the Tech on 2 evenings per week. It'll be hard work ... the real value is the combination of theory and practical work hence the name, sandwich scheme. We pay you a basic wage which gives you some independence. What do you think, Alec?"

"I'm impressed but is there some written qualification at the end, Grant?"

"Oh yes, there will be exams throughout the course to monitor progress. If you pass all those, you will be awarded the equivalent of an ordinary degree. The big difference is that, if you make the grade, you are an immediate asset to the company. Your progress depends on your enthusiasm and ambition. Any other questions, Alec?"

"None whatsoever, I'd like to apply for the scheme, Grant, what's the next step?"

"Get yourself a pair of overalls and report to me on Monday morning, 8am sharp."

"Gee, Grant, that surprised me, so quick. Thanks."

"Welcome aboard, Alec, I just know that you'll take full advantage of the scheme."

Alec waited outside North British until Sarah finished her shift He was smiling broadly as she approached him. "You look like the cat who got the cream, Alec. Tell me all."

"I start work at North British on Monday, Sarah. Your uncle has confidence in me. I didn't realise he was in a position to hire me. You told me he was just one of the draughtsmen."

"Oh, Alec, I wanted you be relaxed when you met him. You're such a worryguts. I didn't want you tongue-tied again. Now, I can tell you he is the company's chief design engineer."

"Jesus, I'm impressed ... he must have been a university graduate."

"Are you kidding? Grant started with the company when he left school at 14. He was what we used to call the tea boy, fetching and carrying, at everybody's beck and call. He stuck to his task and was offered a fitter and turner apprenticeship when he turned 16. He went to night school all through a 5-year apprenticeship and got an engineering diploma. He kept up his studies with a correspondence course and was rewarded as an Associate Member of the Institute of Mechanical Engineers. He has letters after his name, Alec, AMIME. He's a bit of a legend in our family. His achievements as a kid from the wrong side of the tracks were continually being shoved down our throats."

"What a record, Sarah. He came up through the ranks ... now I understand what drives him. Christ, I hope I won't disappoint him."

"You won't, darling man … I'll make sure of that. Don't be so modest, you came up through the ranks too. Now, to more urgent matters … can we get married now?"

"As soon as you can organise it, Sarah."

"And you're happy to let me look after my dad and that other helpless bugger in the Springburn house?"

"Well, it makes sense now. Besides, this helpless bugger is very fond of your dad. So … she who must be obeyed, it's all systems go."

Sarah and Alec were duly married in a private civil ceremony and Alec took up residence in the Springburn house, everything nice, tidy, and legal.

"Well, that's the formalities out of the way, Alec, don't you think it's time to introduce me to your family … get their seal of approval, as it were?"

"Sarah, they will love you. They are dying to meet you. I've already told them how beautiful you are."

"That's nice to know, Alec but regardless of my reception, I love you … that's what's important."

"That is so true, darling. Tomorrow, after your shift, I'll drive you to Bishopbriggs, where all will be revealed. My folks will see immediately that ours is a genuine love match."

Needless to say, Jean and Joe welcomed Sarah into their home, delighted that Alec had found love with a forthright lass of good working-class background. Jean was particularly pleased that Sarah was a cook and lost no time in seeking her assistance in the kitchen, where they really became friends.

Chapter 28

Jim gets demobilised

Jim and Fiona tie the knot
As Jim decides teaching will be his lot.

Jim was called into the office of the compassionate RAMC colonel. "As the war is over, Private MacDonald, you are now eligible for demobilisation. However, I'd like you to consider signing on for another 5 years in the Medical Corps. I know you were studying medicine before you volunteered and, because of your outstanding service, including winning a Military Medal, we are prepared to keep you on the payroll on a Sergeant's wage while you complete your university course, after which we would offer you a commission as Major. What do you say to that, Private?"

"That is an offer which I would have welcomed in the past, Sir, but I'm afraid that I saw enough blood and slaughter in France to last me a lifetime and I shall not be resuming my medical studies."

"Really?" said the surprised Colonel, "what career do you have in mind now?"

"Law, Sir ... I'm thinking of a sedate life practising law."

"Will that be exciting enough for you, Jim?"

"Oh yes, I've had quite enough excitement, Sir."

"Oh well, Jim, in that case, report to our people in Glasgow for the demob formalities, and good luck to you, son."

❧

"Fiona, I have to go to Glasgow to be formally demobilised," said Jim. "While down there I'll be calling into the uni to cancel my medical degree course."

"I know you had reservations about becoming a doctor," said Fiona, "but are you really sure about that, darling?"

"Yes, love, quite sure. Look, in truth, I haven't a clue what I'm going to do. I'll investigate the job market down in the city. The last thing I want is a long engagement for us. I want to marry you as soon as I can afford to. Will you give me two weeks to sort out my affairs, darling?"

"Of course I will, Jim."

"Good, love … If you can get some leave, I'll like you to come down and meet my family."

"OK, sweetheart, that will be no problem … I'll see you in Glasgow in two weeks or thereabouts. I'm looking forward to meeting your mum and sampling her famous cooking."

❧

"Home is the hero," said Jean as she welcomed Jim. "You never told me you'd won a medal. Kirsty Stewart told me in her last letter. Now, wee Hope wants to see it. She's in the kitchen, Jim … do you have the medal with you?"

"Yes, Mum, I have everything with me. Let's get it over with."

"Oh, Jim, you make it sound like a chore. You should be proud … I am, both my boys with medals."

Jean began to cry but Jim cuddled her, "Please don't cry, Mum, I'll behave myself … let's go and see the wee lassie."

As he entered the kitchen, Hope's eyes lit up, "Uncle Jim, show me your medal."

"Here it is, Hope ... I brought it home for you. It's yours to keep."

"Mine to keep," squealed Hope, "does he mean it, Nana?"

Jean laughed, "He does, Hope. He brought it home especially for you. Now, you take it to your room and put it in your treasure chest. Then come back to the kitchen ... we have some cooking to do."

"I half-expected that Jeremy would be here, Mum," said Jim.

"Grace has gone to pick him up at the station. We all call him Jem now. They will be here shortly. Go and make yourself comfortable in the living room.

"Ah, Jim, you beat me to it," said Jem.

"It's lovely to have you home at last, Jim," said Grace, "safe and sound. Joe will be home in a wee while, with Kate. I'm going to the kitchen now to see that the assistant chef is behaving herself. I just can't keep her out of the kitchen but your mum loves her and doesn't mind."

"What's happening with Kate, Grace?"

"Well, she has legally changed her surname to Lennox because she says that Joe Lennox has always been like a father to her."

"That doesn't surprise me, Grace. I expect Joe is quite happy about that. Apart from that, what else has she been up to?"

"Well, she enrolled in the Royal Scottish Academy of Music in the city, where Joe takes her and collects her daily. He is very proud of her. We'll talk later. I'll leave you with my man ... Jem, the gem of my life."

"You are one lucky man, Jem," said Jim, "married to a beautiful talented woman, with a grand wee daughter, chock-full of personality, and baby Malcolm, who'll probably live up to his regal name. Now, I have something to tell you."

"Oh, Jimmy, Jimmy, let me guess ... You have changed your mind again and don't want to be a lawyer. Am I right?"

"Jesus, Jem, is there no end to your prescience? How in hell did you divine that?"

"Well, I read all your so-called scribblings from the sanitorium and I knew that there was no way you would ever be happy as a staid, sober lawyer like me, so the question remains, what do you really want to be?"

"In a word, Jem, I want to be a married man. Everything else pales into insignificance."

"Do you still value my advice, Jim?"

"How could I not? You are my guru."

"I'd like you to consider English teaching as a career, Jim."

"It has never entered my head, standing before a class, most of whom can't wait for the period to end."

"Jim, with your obvious love of poetry and literature, I know that you would get through to some of the class. That would be satisfying. It may even be catching."

"Possibly, but I can't wait to be qualified. I've read an ad for an assistant greenkeeper at my old alma mater, Allan Glen's. I have an interview tomorrow."

"Well, I am taken aback, Jim. You really are determined to get any kind of paid employment, aren't you? So be it … let me know how you go."

The following morning Jim was at the Bishopbriggs playing fields of Allan Glen's school half an hour before his appointment with the head greenkeeper.

The principal of the school, Adrian Gilfillan, Jim's old mentor, happened to be on a routine visit to the playing fields and spotted Jim as he arrived. "Well, this is a pleasant surprise. Jim MacDonald, what brings you here this morning?"

"I'm applying for the vacancy on the ground staff, Sir."

The principal laughed. "I think you may be a bit over-qualified, Jim. By the way, you can drop the Sir title. Please call me Adrian. Now, as I recall, you were studying medicine before you joined the army. You were a brilliant scholar and won a scholarship to the university. I know all about your war record … now you are home, why aren't you taking up where you left off?"

"Oh, it's a long story, Sir ... sorry, Adrian. I want to get married and I need some sort of job to support my wife. In addition, my wartime experiences in the Royal Army Medical Corps turned me off the idea of becoming a doctor."

"I see ... it seems such a shame, Jim. I remember you more than any other former pupil. You stood out, well above the lave. You had a way with words and I always thought you would have made an ideal teacher of English."

"I still love poetry and literature, Adrian. My brother-in-law, only yesterday, asked me if I'd ever considered teaching. He'd been reading some of my stuff and was impressed."

"Well, as a teacher, Jim, you would have the opportunity and the time to continue your writing. Now, tell me, do you have a rooted objection to the idea of teaching?"

"Not really, but I'd have to resume my scholarship on a different path. I'd still have no money to support a wife."

"I may have solved your problem, Jim. The Scottish Education Department, short of teachers, particularly English teachers, has just advertised for people like yourself a free course in teaching at Glasgow university. Furthermore, they will pay successful applicants ten pounds per week. Jim, that's double the wage of an assistant greenkeeper. Now, forget this morning's interview. Make haste to the uni and apply. You are exactly the type they seek. To help ensure your acceptance, I shall telephone the relevant authority at the Department and personally recommend you. Good luck, James MacDonald. I have every faith in you and sincerely hope that one day you will inspire our young at Allan Glen's with the glories of English literature.

To each his own, James."

Two days later, Jim resumed his university career, this time as a student teacher.

He telephoned Fiona and told her all that had occurred. "It means we can be married but you would have to leave your position at the sanitorium. How to you feel about that, my love?"

"To be with you means more to me than nursing. Still, I'm sure that I could transfer to a Glasgow hospital. After all, two wages are better than one."

"That's music to my ears, Fiona. When you can get away to meet my family, we can look for a post for you and a flat for us."

"Jim, why don't you organise a civil ceremony as soon as possible? Keep quiet about it, just let me know when you confirm the date and I'll come running, darling. Meet me at the train station, then, hey presto, you will be able to introduce me as your wife. Is that too daring for you, sweetheart?"

"Not at all, my love, I ought to have thought of that myself. A secret wedding ... how romantic. I like it."

"If we have to, we can have a church wedding later, with everyone invited, including my parents. That ought to soothe any hurt feelings."

Despite advising Jim to keep their plans secret, Fiona decided to tell her mother the whole story. "It will be more convenient for Jim's family if I meet them as his wife."

"Yes, Fiona," laughed her mother, "I can see that ... Jean will only have to allocate one room while you stay there."

"You don't mind missing a simple ceremony, do you, Mum? Jim has a paying job at the uni and I want to find a Glasgow hospital quickly to continue my training so that we'll be able to rent a flat."

"Darling, I don't mind in the slightest. You are showing great initiative and I'm proud of you. Now, it so happens that I have a great business relationship with the chief medical officer at Stobhill Hospital, a really good teaching hospital in Springburn, Glasgow. They do similar work with civilians that you have been doing with the military at the sanitorium. I'll contact him and, by tomorrow, I'm sure I'll be able to say that my clever daughter will have a position waiting for her at Stobhill."

Chapter 29

The gathering of the clan
All going to plan

The extended family were at the Lennox household, awaiting the arrival of Jim and his fiancée. It was late afternoon when they turned up. As everyone shouted welcome, Jim said, "Listen everybody, I have an announcement to make. Fiona and I are newlyweds. We were married an hour ago in the Glasgow Registry Office. We just couldn't wait any longer. Now, let the introductions commence, starting with my mother and Joe, but is there any chance of a wee cuppa tea while you all get to know Fiona? I'm parched."

"I'll get that for you, uncle Jim, and one for your lovely bride," said wee Hope.

On hearing that, Grace sat at the piano and launched into a swinging version of 'Here comes the bride'. Everyone joined in the chorus, whereupon Fiona burst into tears. Jean was concerned and rushed to her side. "No, no, I'm fine, Mrs Lennox ... I'm just overcome with the spontaneous welcome. I couldn't be happier."

"Oh Fiona, why would you not be welcome? Not only are you my younger son's wife, you are also the daughter of one of my special friends, your mother, Kirsty. I too couldn't be happier."

"I hope you weren't upset, Mum," said Jim, "by missing out on a wedding invitation."

Jean laughed, "I'm getting used to it. Jem and Grace, Alec and Sarah, and now, you and Fiona. It's become a family tradition. Now, as soon as everybody's been introduced there's a smorgasbord waiting in the dining room. Thanks to a thoughtful gift from Sarah, a fellow cook, the food is kept hot and separate in a bain marie, a very useful addition when we have a large dinner party like tonight. OK, family, grab a plate and help yourself. There's roast beef, lamb, chicken, and a selection of fresh vegetables from the garden. Wee Hope and I have been busy so, when we're all seated at the extended table, we can get started."

"Just before we eat," said Joe, "I'd like to say a few words."

"Only a few, Gramps," said wee Hope, "we don't want the food to get cold."

Everyone laughed at the pertinacity of the assistant cook, precocious well beyond her years.

"Don't worry, Hope, I'll keep it short. I just want to say that we've been blessed that all of the family survived the war and I personally welcome Fiona, who is already loved, as the latest addition to my extended family. Now, tuck in and enjoy."

After dinner, they all assembled in the lounge, to hear Kate play the piano. Joe, her keenest admirer, said, "What are you going to favour us with this evening, Kate?"

"My favourite piece at the moment is Rainbow Prelude, by Chopin."

"That sounds a bit high falutin', Kate," said Alec.

"Well, I'll start it, but if it's too highbrow, just sing out and I'll switch to something else."

Wee Hope turned and admonished the assembly. "Don't any of you dare. Auntie Kate always plays beautiful tunes."

Everyone laughed and Joe said, "I agree with wee Hope. Kate can do no wrong. Let's hear your favourite piece, Kate."

The Prelude was greeted with applause, even from Alec, an acknowledged musical Philistine.

"Now, Dad, I shall play your favourite, Beethoven's Moonlight Sonata."

"That will be lovely, Kate, although you know it makes me cry, it's so beautiful."

Sure enough, Joe was wiping his eyes as the last poignant note lingered in the air.

"To finish, I'll surprise everyone with something cheery," said Kate.

So saying, she launched into the Beer Barrel Polka, which was met with rapturous applause.

"You didn't learn that at the Academy, Kate," said Grace.

Kate merely smiled demurely and said, "My wonderful first teacher will now, I hope, consent to entertain you."

Grace took over, playing quiet background music, allowing the family to get acquainted with Fiona.

Fiona announced that she already had a job lined up at Stobhill Hospital.

"Well, what do you know," said Sarah, "That's in Springburn, not far from us."

"Yes," said Jim, "and tomorrow we'll be out, bright and early, looking for a flat."

"It so happens, Jim," said Sarah, "that there is a wee house to rent at the end of our street, right on the tramline. If Springburn is a suitable location for both of you, it could save you a lot of time searching around. The only drawback is there's no garage, just like our place."

"That wouldn't matter, Sarah," said Jim, "We wouldn't need a car. From what you say, Fiona is a stone's throw from Stobhill and can walk to work and I'll take the tram to the university."

Jean overheard the conversation and relayed the contents to Joe. "You are so right, Joe. We are truly blessed. All is well with our extended family and, God willing, a bright, peaceful future lies ahead."

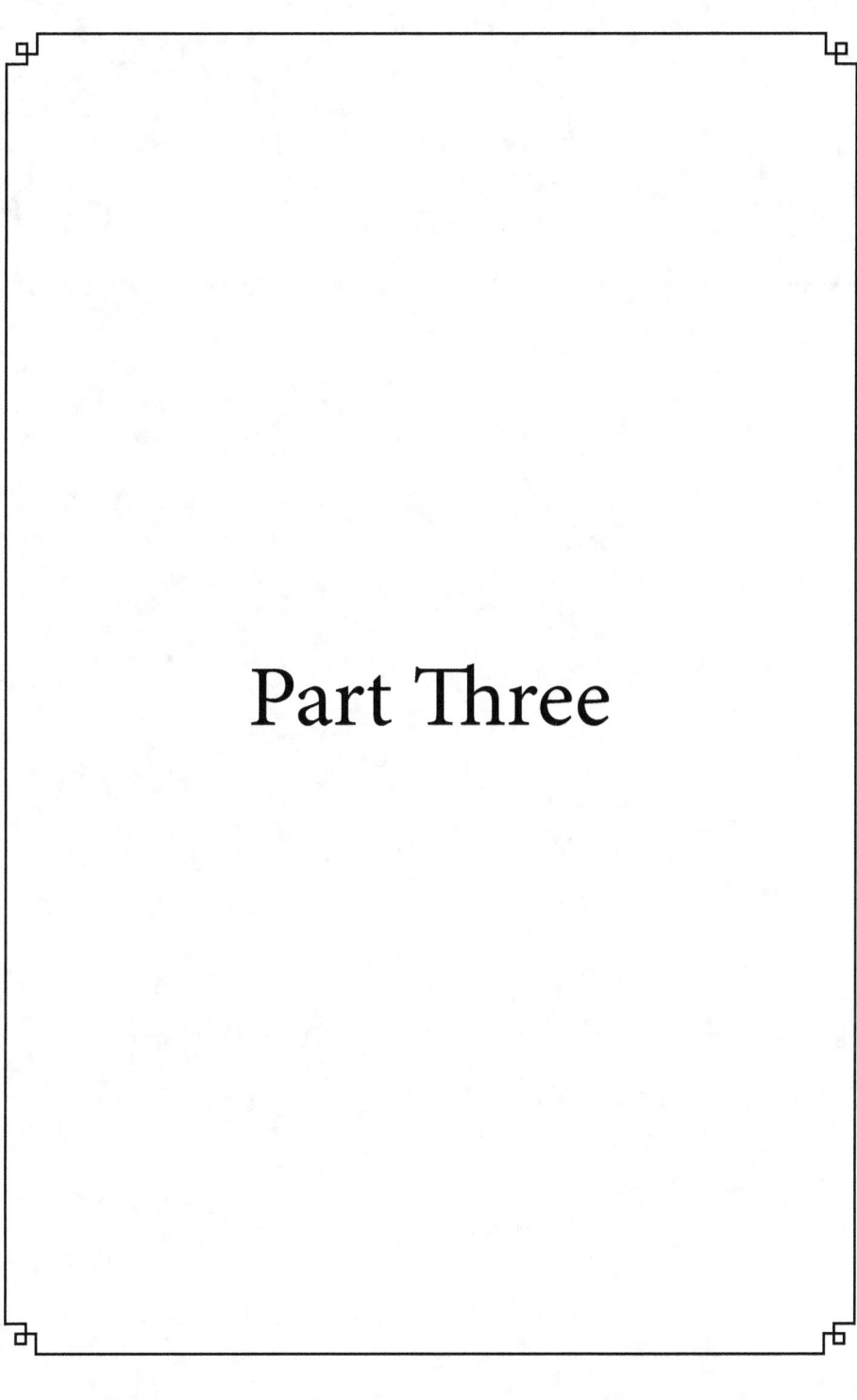

Part Three

Chapter 30

*Kate decides the classics are not her thing
As she converts to jazz and swing.*

*I*n mid-1948, Jim excelled at Glasgow University, graduating as the best of his group. As a result, he was given the choice of high schools which were in need of an English teacher. He naturally discussed this with Fiona, who was now a qualified nurse at Stobhill Hospital, seemingly happy there. To his surprise, she asked if Inverness High School was on the list.

"Yes, it is, darling, but I've been thinking of schools down here, so that you could continue your nursing without having to relocate again. You obviously have something on your mind, so tell me, Fiona, what's going on."

"Several things, Jim ... Nursing was never a must have career for me. It was just a way of doing my bit during the war. Now that you are a qualified teacher, I feel the need to start a family of our own. I'd also like to get you away from smoky old industrial Glasgow, back to the pure air of the Highlands, which restored you to full health. We could be close to my parents, who would be only too willing to help if I need a hand with the baby. So, have you any objections to living in Inverness, my love?"

"Fiona, wherever you'll be happy, I'll be happy too. I'll set the wheels in motion right away."

"Good, darling, I'll ask Mum to look for a house to rent. I have a good feeling about this, Jim. I'll get a job up there until the birth is in sight."

Jim laughed, "You seem to have it all planned, lass. I suppose you have a couple of names picked out for the bairn already."

"I have, Jim, and I have a fair idea when the bairn will be born. You see, darling, I'm three months pregnant already. I should have told you but I just wanted to be sure. Are you mad at me, Jim?"

"I'm absolutely delighted, sweetheart, and I know that Joe and my mother will be over the moon ... another wee addition to their extended family."

In 1949, Kate was 20 years old. Her dedication to the piano was as strong as ever but she was having second thoughts about a classical career. She had struck up a friendship with Sam Donohue, who had introduced her to another musical world. He played clarinet and was one of the tutors at the Royal Scottish academy of Music. He had escorted her one Saturday afternoon to the Barrowland Ballroom in the east end of the city. The featured band was an Australian group led by a pianist named Graham Bell. Kate watched his keyboard technique and could tell that he had been classically trained. However, it was the music they were playing that had Kate entranced. "What is this stuff?" she said, "I've never heard anything quite like it."

"It's known as New Orleans Revival, Kate. New Orleans jazz began in the twenties but was superseded in the forties by the big swing bands, playing written arrangements. You must have heard records of Glenn Miller and Tommy Dorsey."

"Yes, I have, but they didn't have the same effect on me as this group."

"These Aussie guys are bringing back polyphonic music, with all the musos improvising on the spot, around the theme. The same thing is happening in London, with Humphrey Lyttleton, an old Etonian from an English aristocratic family leading the way. He was hooked on it the first time he heard Louis Armstrong's Hot Five's recordings from 1926."

"Whatever it is called, Sam, it's very exciting ... I love it. I reckon I'm hooked on it too."

"Good, Kate, because it's a breath of fresh air among the bland pop tunes of today."

"Do you play this music, Sam?"

"Not exactly, but I've just started up a small group playing traditional jazz. I find that exciting."

"Really? I'd like to hear it, Sam."

"Well, come to my place on Saturday afternoon. We'll be rehearsing then for a gig at the university on Saturday night. I live in Bishopbriggs too, so you could walk to my joint. I'll look forward to seeing you there, Kate."

"Kate, welcome to our humble abode," said Sam. "Meet my better half, Billie. Billie, this is young Kate Lennox, a prodigy on the piano, if I ever heard one."

"How are you, Kate?" said Billie. "Sam tells me you are a classical pianist, destined for a great future."

"Oh, Billie, I'm not so sure about that now. My taste in music is changing."

"Sam tells me that you have perfect pitch, which is a rarity in musicians. I wish I could lay claim to that."

"Oh ... So, Billie, you are a musician?"

"Yes, Kate, I play double bass. I also sing a bit when required. My father named me Billie, after the great Billie Holiday. He was an ardent fan of her singing."

"Kate, come and meet our drummer," said Sam, "We pinched him from the local pipe band, as he's been converted to jazz. This is Danny Bruce, who really swings. OK, that's the formalities over, let's play."

Sam led the others into a moderately-paced rendition of a popular song, 'Memories of You'. He didn't deviate from the written melody and then nodded to Billie, who sang the lyric in a pleasantly husky voice, also sticking to the composer's melody. However, when Sam took over, he improvised, creating jazz on the spot.

As the band put in a big finish, Kate applauded enthusiastically. "That was great, I loved the idea of the straight intro and Billie's singing but the exciting improvisation at the finish was what that Australian group were doing. I'm hooked, people, please play some more."

"We will, Kate, but listen to this record of an American trio, playing their version of that song."

The lead clarinettist weaved round the melody from the start, partnered by a pianist playing obligato, creating counter melodies in sympathy with the leader. The drummer played soft brushes in a steady rhythm. Those three musicians, to Kate's ears, were magic.

"That was out of this world, Sam. Who are these guys?"

"That was the Benny Goodman Trio. Did you like the piano man, Kate?"

"He was phenomenal. I wish I could play like that, Sam. Who is he?

"That's Teddy Wilson, a black pianist, invited by the Jewish Benny Goodman, against all advice, to join his group. Benny tolerated no racism in music ... he wanted the best."

"Now, Kate," said Billie, "you can understand what's missing in our group ... a piano player."

"That's right, Kate," said Sam, "in a very short time, with a bit of practice, you could play like that. We need you!"

When the trio left for their university gig, Kate went home with a list of their repertoire. Sam had told her that she was probably familiar with most of their tunes, as they were popular melodies, played conventionally on radio by the dance bands of the day. In addition, Sam had given her records of the jazz classics with which she may not be familiar. When she arrived home, she went straight to the piano and began to play the pop tunes on the list. Grace heard her and wondered why Kate was deviating from practising the classics.

"What's all this, Kate? I'm pretty sure this isn't Academy homework."

Kate laughed and told Grace the whole story. "I've been invited to play piano in a small jazz group and I'm very keen to accept. They want me to improvise round the melody like Teddy Wilson."

"Teddy Wilson! I think they are a wee bit ambitious, Kate. He's the tops."

"I know, I have him on a few records here."

"Well, Kate, if your heart is set on this, I can help you."

"How, Grace? We only have one piano."

"I know every song on your list. I'll sing or hum the melody and you can do your Teddy Wilson obligatos to the best of your ability."

Kate began tentatively, sticking to the chords, but gradually her confidence increased and she began to compose counter melodies, very softly, not overpowering Grace's voice. After half a dozen songs, Grace called a halt. "It's kitchen time for me, Kate. That's enough for tonight."

"Oh, Grace, you must have some comment ... am I wasting my time with this?"

"On the contrary, lass. I'd say you are a natural. You have a feeling for jazz and, although you're no Teddy Wilson ... yet, you'll meet the needs of your Glasgow group ... that's for sure. Now, Kate, don't you think you ought to have a wee talk with your dad about this? After all, he's been your biggest supporter in your classical training."

"I will, Grace, and if he's not happy about this, I'll drop the whole idea. He means more to me than any personal ambitions I may have."

"Dad," said Kate, "could I have a wee chat with you before our evening meal?"

"Kate, of course you may ... I'm available for you anytime you like. By the way, I just heard Grace singing. Was she also playing the piano or was that you?"

"That was me, Dad ... that's what I want to talk to you about. I've been invited to play piano in a jazz quartet. You heard me practising their repertoire instead of the classical homework. Have you any comment?"

"Only that you sounded great, Kate. I didn't realise that you could play like that. I've always loved jazz and swing but I was hopeless when I tried it. When can I hear your quartet?"

"Oh, Dad, you never cease to amaze me. I thought you'd be angry with me for neglecting my proper studies."

"Kate, Kate, all I ever tried to do was to help you to learn to play piano properly. I never expected you to become a concert pianist. You've already exceeded my expectations so, if playing in a jazz band will make you happy, then I'll be happy too. To each his own, Kate. That's always been my philosophy in life. Can I just offer one bit of advice, though?"

"Yes, Dad, and I'll will act on it, whatever it is."

"Good, Kate. I think you have the ability to play jazz and finish your classical course too. You have less than a year to graduate. Get those letters after your name.

You will find the qualification useful later if circumstances change and you decide to take up teaching."

"Consider it done, Dad."

"Good girl, now, when can I hear your quartet?"

"On Saturday afternoon, Dad, come with me to their rehearsal. I know that you will enjoy the music."

"I have a better idea, Kate. Invite your friends to come here where they can hear you on our baby grand and realise how much you have progressed."

"Oh, Dad, I'm glad you suggested that. The group only has a tinny upright piano, sadly out of tune."

Chapter 31

1950

Joe decides he will step down
And Jeremy accepts the crown.

On July 6th, in Inverness, Fiona MacDonald, now a full-time housewife, gave birth to a healthy baby girl, delivered at home by her mother, Dr Kirsty Stewart.

The proud father, Jim, was delighted and suggested that the bairn be named Kirsty, in honour of Fiona's mother.

However, when Fiona advised her mum of Jim's wish, the good doctor thought that would lead to some confusion.

"Jim," said Kirsty, "the choice should be yours and Fiona's but, I would be delighted if your wee lassie was named Jean, after your mother, whom I love like a sister."

And so, it came to pass. Joe and Jean Lennox drove to Inverness for the christening of baby Jean MacDonald, the latest addition to their extended family. After the formalities at the church, Joe had a quiet word with Angus.

"I've been meaning to talk privately about a business matter for some time now, Angus, so this is a good opportunity."

"Nothing wrong, is there, Joe? Things are going well up here in the highlands."

"Yes, I know, Angus, you've done a wonderful job up here, but I have a wee problem … I'm approaching 65 and starting to feel my age. I'm looking for someone to replace me as the national CEO and you are the obvious choice. How do you feel about that?"

"Well, I suppose I ought to feel flattered but I'd have a problem finding someone to replace me up here. Besides, Joe, for family reasons, I would not want to leave Inverness, so I'd have to decline."

Joe smiled, "That's exactly what I thought you'd say, but I had to ask."

"I don't think you'll have much trouble finding a replacement, Joe. You have a standout candidate right on your doorstep."

Surprised, Joe said, "Who are you talking about, Angus?"

"Jeremy Cowan of course. He knows more about the overall operation of the Co-op than anyone on the board."

"You're missing the point, Angus. Jeremy isn't on the board. Strictly speaking, he's not even an employee of the Co-op as I really only have him on contract."

"That's as may be, Joe, but all that can be overcome if you think he's the right man for the job."

"Well, my friend," said Joe, "you've certainly given me something to think about."

Early in 1950, Billie Donohue fell pregnant and was having a difficult time. Sam reluctantly disbanded the group as all of his free time was now devoted to caring for his wife.

Although disappointed, Kate could now concentrate completely on her classical studies and by mid-year graduated with flying colours. She was duly congratulated by Phyllis Petrie, Director of the Royal Scottish Academy of Music.

"Thank you, Phyllis. I've enjoyed my time here and I'm indebted to the Academy for the unstinting support and from you, in particular."

"Until a few months ago, I was certain that I'd be sending you to the London Conservatorium of Music for a post-graduate course," said Phyllis. "I was convinced that you had the touch of genius necessary to become a successful concert pianist. However, I heard on the grapevine that your music ambitions had led you in another direction. Would you care to confirm that, Kate?"

"Yes, Phyllis, I have been smitten by a form of music in which one can create new melodies on the spot. You probably know it's called jazz. I've discovered that, rather than play Mozart or Beethoven classics, I've already experienced the thrill of improvisation."

"I see," said Phyllis, "and according to what I hear, Kate, you have been putting that touch of genius to good effect in your chosen genre. Your friends tell me you could be another Teddy Wilson ... high praise indeed."

"Friends tend to exaggerate, Phyllis. I have a long way to go to get anywhere near his class."

"Well, that's as may be, but now you have graduated from the Academy, what are your immediate plans, Kate?"

"As my jazz group has wound up, I suppose I'll have to think about taking in kids as pupils who mostly don't really want to be there. I'm sure you know what I mean. Phyllis."

"Only too well, Kate ... over-ambitious mothers with too much money. Now, I can help you avoid that path."

"Tell me more, Phyllis ... I'm all ears."

"The London Conservatorium of Music is searching for a top-class pianist to join their teaching staff," said Phyllis, "and I've taken the liberty of submitting your name. Kate, the job is yours, on a 2-year contract, if you want it. There's a studio flat on the premises, with a peppercorn rent, if you accept. They trust my judgement, Kate. Think about it, you'll be in the heart of London, where your jazz is all happening. Furthermore, you'll be teaching young people of real talent, so I'm sure you'll get a kick out of that."

"That's an offer too good to refuse, Phyllis. Will you let them know I accept?"

"Yes, Kate, I'll set it all up. They will advise you of your starting date."

"I'll keep in touch, Phyllis and can't thank you enough."

As soon as Joe returned from Inverness, he contacted Jem. "I've been meaning to ask you for some time now ... How is your project going at the Gorbals?"

"It's been disappointing, Joe. I was going to act the knight in shining armour, helping the underprivileged whom I remembered from my youth there but the post-war boom has seen a remarkable change in the fortunes of the residents. That's great for them and I'm happy for them but I now find myself seriously under-employed."

"Ah well, times change, Jem, not always for the better either. I have a new proposition for you, in the light of what you've just told me. I'd like you to work full-time as an employee of CWS. You can still hang on to your Gorbals office for the bits and pieces that may come your way but I have ambitions for you in the year ahead to become a board member of the Co-Op."

"Joe, Joe, I willingly accept your offer to work for you full-time but you may meet some resistance from the other board members about promoting me."

"You are wrong there, Jem ... the other members are well aware of your contribution to the success of our enterprise. They will welcome you with open arms."

"Well, that's nice to hear but what's really on your mind here, Joe?"

"Jem, by the end of the year, I want you to take over my job. I'm ready to hang up my boots."

"Christ, I can hardly believe what I'm hearing here. You're Joe Lennox, a legend in the community. How can I replace you?"

"Oh, Jem, ask Jean, ask Grace, ask Angus Stewart. You'll fill the bill all right. Now that Kate has left the nest, Jean and I are going to buy a wee place in Cadder, a wee village not too far away. You and your family will have this grand old house, rent-free, courtesy of the Co-Op, to raise your lovely bairns."

Chapter 32

As Jem assumes the Co-Op crown,
Kate heads south to London Town

"*K*ate Lennox, my name is Keith Scott. I'm the guy you come to if you have any queries or problems. Welcome to the Conservatorium."

"Thank you, Keith. This is a great opportunity for me and I'm grateful. I hope I can justify my selection."

"You know, you are the youngest tutor we've ever had but you come with such high credentials, courtesy of my old friend Phyllis Petrie, that we have every faith in you."

"That's kind of you, Keith ... I really don't know how to respond."

"I'm told," said Keith, "that your taste in music is ... shall we say, eclectic."

Kate smiled, "I'd guess that Phyllis has told you that I'm into jazz ... right?"

"Yes, and as long as you do your job here, there's no reason why you can't spend your spare time taking advantage of the London jazz scene."

"You have no objection, Keith?"

"How could I, Kate? ... I play double bass occasionally at Baker Street with Humphrey Lyttleton's group. If you like, I'll take you there on Saturday evening and introduce you as a top piano player and a fellow trad jazz enthusiast."

"Well, this is a much more exciting introduction to life in London than I could have hoped for," said Kate. "I'll look forward to Saturday evening."

"Humph, this young lady is Kate Lennox, a classically-trained pianist, now part of our team at the Conservatorium. Kate, meet Humphrey Lyttelton."

"Hello, Kate, are you just slumming or do you like jazz?"

Kate laughed, "I'm certainly not slumming. I love jazz and have played with a small group in Glasgow. You have a great sound here, New Orleans revival, right?"

"Yes, mostly ... is that the sort of stuff you played in darkest Scotland, Kate?"

"Not really, we played Benny Goodman-type jazz."

"I'd love to hear you play, Kate," said Humph. "Perhaps you and Keith can entertain us at the break?"

Kate looked inquisitively at Keith, who nodded and said, "That's fine, Humph, we'll work out some tunes we both know. I haven't heard Kate play either but I have the feeling we will cope."

At the break, Humph and his group repaired to the bar and Keith led Kate on to the stage. They had decided to surprise Humph by playing a New Orleans traditional song, 'When my dreamboat comes home'. Kate played the melody at medium tempo, then signalled to Keith to take over on double bass while she quietly played chords.

From that point, she improvised and people began to get up and dance. A young man with a clarinet in hand rose and asked Kate if he could join in. She nodded enthusiastically and they had a swinging trio. Shortly, the house band drummer joined them and doubled the tempo. Clarinet and piano alternated with exciting solos. The quartet put in a big finish to rapturous applause from the audience.

Humph gave them the thumbs up and the impromptu quartet played a few Benny Goodman standards before the three guests relinquished their places, having entertained the audience for over half an hour.

"Well, Kate, you certainly laid them in the aisles," said Humph. "My drummer couldn't wait to join you. You really swing."

"That's kind of you, but the young clarinet man ... Jesus, he was fabulous."

"That's Sandy Brown. Like you, he's a recent arrival in London from Edinburgh ... yes, he's one of your lot from the north. He has already assembled a group down here, playing New Orleans stuff. They are just getting started but I expect you'll hear a lot more about him. He left right after your contribution, having a gig lined up later tonight at a nearby pub. Do you have a card, Kate?"

"Not yet, but I'll have some printed by next Saturday. I'll drop one in."

"Good," said Humph, "I'm sure you'll be in great demand by then. Sandy Brown will be here too. Perhaps he will have time to introduce himself properly to you."

When Keith drove her back to her flat, he said, "You had a great time tonight, didn't you, Kate?"

"I sure did, Keith, and I'm grateful to you for the introduction to Humphrey Lyttleton."

"Next week, I won't be with you, Kate. As a married man with three kids, I can only get out to play jazz at night once a month but I'm sure you can cope on your own from now on."

"Sure, no problem, Keith. I know they will make me welcome there."

Next Saturday, a short bus ride dropped Kate right outside the Baker Street jazz club.

Humph and his band were in full stride and Kate sat back, enjoying the New Orleans tunes, learning as she listened.

Sandy Brown arrived and sat down beside her and formally introduced himself, apologising for rushing away the week before. "I believe you are a classically-trained pianist, Kate."

"Yes, and I teach piano at the Conservatorium but I've become very fond of jazz."

"No doubt you're a good sight-reader, is that right?"

"Without boasting, I can say yes, Sandy, better than most. I also learned early in my training that I have perfect pitch."

"Not many musicians can lay claim to that, Kate. That is a great attribute. Tell me, do you still play the classics?"

"In a word, no, Sandy. I spend most of my free time learning jazz tunes."

"From our short gig last Saturday, I realised that you are the best pianist I've heard, and I know you are going to be inundated with offers."

"That's lovely to hear but I'm committed to a 2-year contract with Keith at the Conservatorium, so going on the road with a band would be impossible for me. Any jobs I get will have to be local."

"I understand, Kate. Do you have a card?"

Kate handed over a card inscribed Kate Lennox, pianist and teacher, with phone number on the bottom. Sandy read it, thanked her, and hoped he could provide her with work from time to time. "There is one problem which you ought to know about, Kate. A lot of the pubs and other venues don't have a piano. If I were you, with your musical talent, I'd learn to play guitar and banjo, portable substitutes for piano in a jazz band. That would open up many more opportunities for you, Kate."

"What a great idea, Sandy, a couple more strings to my bow, as it were. There are instruments to spare at the conservatorium. I'll get started on that straight away."

Sandy laughed at her mixed metaphor. "You realise, in a few months, you'll have to print a new set of cards ... Kate Lennox, musician. Actually, I prefer Katy. Can't you see the future, the Katy Lennox Trio, or the Katy Lennox Quartet?"

Kate laughed, "Sandy, you're doing wonders for my ego. You'd better stick around."

"Well, Humph is calling us to the stage. It appears you, me, and his drummer will be providing the half-time entertainment. You call the tunes and let's show them how it's done, Katy."

Chapter 33

Scotland

To bear a child had been Sarah's obsession,
But alas, she's now in deep depression.

As the end of the year approached, Jem had been on the Co-op board long enough to remove any doubts about his extensive knowledge of all aspects of the company. Consequently, when Joe dropped the bombshell of his retirement and suggested Jeremy Cowan as his successor, no one objected and it was a fait accompli.

"Well, Jem, here we are in this mansion, just our family," said Grace. "It will take a bit of getting used to without Joe, Jean, and Kate."

"You're right, Grace, but Joe was overdue to retire. He'd worked hard all his life and couldn't wait to settle in his cottage in Cadder."

"There is one thing worrying me, Jem. Will you be having business dinners here from now on?"

Jem smiled, "Occasionally, my love ... what are you worried about? You will be an excellent and charming hostess."

"But I can't cook like Jean. She was a wizard, producing courses of fabulous food for large groups of people."

Jem laughed, "You're forgetting your daughter will be there to help."

"Hope!" exclaimed Grace, "God Almighty, Jem, she's still a wee lassie, eleven years old."

"Relax, darling, I'm having a bit of fun with you. Jean has told me she'll be available for such occasions. Her cottage is only 10 minutes away. She's already got her kitchen garden up and running at Cadder. Besides, I've already hired a part-time gardener to tend to this place, so we'll always have plenty fresh vegetables on hand."

"You're a proper villain, Jem. I **was** worried, you know."

"I'm sorry, love. Now, you can concentrate on expanding your piano tutoring, if you're so inclined."

"I will ... after all, with you at work and the kids at school, I'll be all alone during the day. I may as well do something useful and earn a bit of extra money."

In 1952, Alec MacDonald was now in a well-paid management role at North British Locomotive. Sarah suggested that it was time to start a family and Alec enthusiastically agreed. By mid-year, she was pregnant but decided to keep busy working until it was time to prepare for birth. Unfortunately, when she was 6 months pregnant, she suffered a nasty fall and subsequently miscarried. To make matters worse, the doctor informed her that her womb had been damaged and further pregnancy was impossible. Sarah was inconsolable and fell into a deep depression. Alec discussed the situation with his mother and Jean took temporary residence at the Springburn house to help Sarah get through this bad period. Sarah was grateful for her mother-in-law's compassionate understanding and, ultimately, she recovered sufficiently to go back to her canteen job. Alec, however, sensed that it would require much more time for his wife to get over the loss of a passionately desired child.

Chapter 34

Katy forms a winning team,
Living out her music dream.

*H*eeding Sandy Brown's advice, Kate took advantage of the facilities at the Conservatorium to learn guitar and banjo. With her perfect pitch, excellent sight reading, superb two-handed piano skills, and dedicated practice, Kate felt equipped to take her place within 6 months in any small jazz group as a multi-instrumentalist. She had fulfilled her obligatory two years at the Conservatorium but was happy to continue until she was ready to 'hit the road' with a trio or quartet of her own. Meanwhile she was now in constant demand by various small groups, filling in for sick or otherwise engaged members. This was great experience for her, playing in different styles all over the greater London area. She was also building up a healthy bank balance which would be necessary when the time came to leave the Conservatorium to become a full-time jazz musician.

Humphrey Lyttelton ultimately offered her a position in his New Orleans revival group, as did her Scottish advisor, Sandy Brown, but she turned both offers down, explaining that she didn't want to restrict herself to one genre. Both understood but said she'd always be welcome to 'sit in' as a guest artist.

Kate had come a long way in the world of jazz. She had acquired a reputation and was supplementing her income with regular paid gigs.

Sandy Brown, as a fellow Scot, was particularly supportive of her. He suggested that when she decided to form her own band that an all-girls group could be a winner for her. She was intrigued by the idea and asked Sandy to keep an eye open for girls who may be interested.

"A double bass player, a drummer, and a clarinettist ... that's what I have in mind, Sandy."

"The Katy Lennox quartet ... I love it," said Sandy. "Just let me know when you're ready, Katy. I'll have no trouble finding keen lassies who'd love to have such an opportunity. At the present time, the jazz world is very much male orientated."

Two months later, Kate had recruited Anna Frew, on clarinet, tenor sax, and flute, Patsy Jones, on double bass, bass guitar, and vocals, and Donna Rich, on drums.

They gathered at Kate's flat and built up an extensive repertoire of trad jazz and swing. They recorded a demo tape, courtesy of Humphrey Lyttelton, and distributed copies to all the likely venues in the metropolitan area.

Soon, they had enough regular gigs to make a living ... Saturday afternoons, Saturday evenings, Sunday afternoons and Sunday evenings, plus a regular gig on Wednesday evenings. At this stage, Kate could hang on to her job and flat. She kitted out the quartet with smart matching uniforms and their attractive appearance, allied with the professionalism of their music, spread their fame beyond greater London.

To Kate's dismay, her girls were not keen on spending any time away from home as their male companions disapproved. Their sex life was more important than their music so Kate had to turn down lucrative gigs in Manchester and Liverpool.

Ultimately, Kate handed over the leadership of the group to Anna Frew and decided to seek pastures new. She filled in some time as guest of Humphrey who repeated his offer of a full-time job. Again, she turned him down and he said, "Kate, you could write your own ticket to any band in the country but I feel you're searching for something different ... am I right?"

"As usual, Humph, you put your finger on it. My all-girls band can carry on without me but I can now fulfil a desire to go where jazz began without feeling guilty at deserting them. Yes, I want to go to America. Have you any suggestions how I can go about it?"

"How about a trip to New York on the Mauretania cruise ship ... does that appeal, Kate?"

"It sounds expensive, Humph ... what's on your mind?"

"I was at Eton with a chap who is now a big wheel in the Cunard Line. He's always asking me to help him finding entertainment for the passengers. Here's his number. Ring him and I'll guarantee he makes you an offer."

A few days later, Kate rang Humph to thank him. "It's all set, Humph, I'll soon be on my way on the Mauretania. I don't know what my duties will be yet. Your friend simply made an offer I couldn't refuse. You must have praised me to the skies."

"I just told him the truth, Kate. Look, I'm sorry your all-girls group didn't work out for you."

"Well, I learned a lesson. The girls weren't free agents like me."

"I'm surprised that some chap hasn't snapped up a good-looker like you, Kate. I expect you'll fall for someone and get married before long."

"Not likely, Humph, I'm married to my career, wherever it leads me."

As she hung up the phone, Kate reflected on the fact that she had never been sexually attracted to any of the men she had met. Although she had automatically dismissed Humph's marriage forecast, she now wondered whether there was something unnatural about her single-mindedness. Finally, she shrugged the idea off, convincing herself that the right guy hadn't come along yet.

Chapter 35

An eventful trip lies in store,
As Katy leaves her native shore.

As she boarded the Mauretania, she was greeted warmly by the entertainment officer. "Welcome, Katy Lennox. My name is Neville Fraser but everyone calls me Nifty. I've been told that we're very lucky to have you. We have a dance band who play in the evenings for the after-dinner dancers. I hope you can play piano during their breaks ... how does that sound, Katy?"

"No problem there, Nifty ... is that all?"

"Not quite ... I've slotted you into the after-lunch hour for the tea-dance. I'm told your preference is jazz but are you happy to play the odd waltz for the elderly folk?"

Katy laughed, "Nifty, I'm versatile ... you pay the piper so you call the tune."

Nifty Nev breathed a sigh of relief. "I'm so glad you're not one of those prima donnas. I can see that we're going to get along just fine."

"Of course we will, Nifty. By the way, I also play banjo and guitar. If your dance band is ever a man short in that department, I'm happy to fill in. No extra charge, I just love to play music, OK?"

"Right, let's get you settled in and then I'll show you round the ship, if you like."

As the pair strolled along the deck, a tall young man in shorts and T-shirt came jogging towards them and said, "Hi, Nifty, who's the beautiful doll?"

"Russ, this young lady is Katy Lennox, who has just joined us from London. Katy, meet Russ Lennox, the leader of our dance band."

"Gee, I hope we're not related," said Russ, grinning and making eyes at Katy. "I'll bet you two bob I can kiss you without touching you."

Without waiting for a response, he wrapped his arms around her and planted a long kiss on her lips. Katy struggled free of his grasp and spluttered, "But you touched me!"

"That's right, doll ... and here's your two bob. Now, I must finish my morning run. No doubt I'll see you later."

"Well, Nifty," expostulated Katy, "he's a bit too pushy for my liking."

"He surprised me, Katy ... he's not normally like that with other girls. I reckon he must like you."

Nifty had allocated her a really nice cabin all to herself. She had expected to be down near the steerage beside the crew so she surmised that Humph had a hand in this. She fervently hoped that he hadn't overplayed her talents. As she prepared for her first lunchtime job, she reflected on the audacity of Russ Lennox. Despite her initial outrage, she was no longer offended. After all, the man was an Adonis, handsome enough to double for Clark Gable, currently the top movie star. Apart from his looks, for the first time in her life, she had been stirred physically by his confident approach, especially the lingering kiss. She glanced at the two-shilling piece and decided to hang on to it for a while, until she found out what developed with the bold Mr Lennox.

Nifty arrived and escorted her to lunch in the first-class dining saloon. "Am I entitled to lunch here, Nifty?"

"Of course, Katy, but I can tell you that you are the first paid musician ever to be granted that privilege."

"I'm flummoxed, mate ... why me?"

"Because I signed you on as a first-class passenger and put you in a first-class cabin."

"Oh, God, your friend, Mr Lyttelton, I presume?"

"Katy, just let's say that family carries a lot of weight. Humph assured me you'd be worth every penny but, if you fail, he will personally pay your passage."

On hearing this, Katy had a resurgence of confidence. "Nifty you won't have a worry in the world. As the jazzmen say, I'll lay 'em in the aisles."

There were over three hundred people being served lunch when Katy got up to play. There was much conversation as one would expect so she decided to indulge herself in some quiet background music. What better choice than a few Chopin études?

She glanced at Nifty and smiled as she saw the surprised look on his face.

After a while, she became aware that at many tables, people had stopped talking and were listening intently to the beautiful melodies. Encouraged, she upped the volume and played her father's favourite piece, Beethoven's Moonlight Sonata. Although there was a ripple of applause from the older people, she decided that it was time to perform her real duty and cater for the tea-dancers.

By the time she'd played the Cole Porter repertoire, the dance area was crowded and there was enthusiastic applause after every number she played from then on. Finally, she was confident enough to test her audience with some of her favourite New Orleans classic jazz and was thrilled to see old and young swaying to the infectious rhythm.

All too soon, it was over and Nifty could not wipe the smile off his face. He announced that Miss Katy Lennox could be heard later in the evening. This was received with smiles and acclamation. "Well, Katy, what can I say? You were brilliant and you'll have a full house tonight."

Nifty was right. Katy went an hour early to the dining salon to hear the band for the first time. Every seat was occupied so she stood at the bar. Russ Lennox was singing in a pleasant baritone voice one of the pop songs of the day. He looked good in a tuxedo and sounded like a cross between Bing Crosby and Perry Como.

When the song ended, he came to the bar. "Hi, doll, I'm glad you came early."

"Well, I wanted to hear the band but I'm very impressed by your voice."

"Really, doll? ... It's only commercial stuff. I only sing 'cos none of the others can. Anyway, I want to show you our play list. There are 30 tunes we'll play tonight, so I'd like you to avoid them when you come on, OK doll?"

"No problem, Russ, I have my own list."

"Could you play 30 minutes at our first break? My mob like to have a smoke and a drink and we're usually rushed by Nifty to get back on stage."

"I'll fill in as long as you need, Russ. Just come back when you're ready."

Russ looked doubtful as he returned to lead the band on clarinet.

Nifty arrived as the band prepared to take their break. "Hi, Nifty," said Katy. "Russ seems a bit worried that this doll won't cut the mustard."

"Jesus Christ, is he in for a shock!"

As the band was leaving, Nifty announced, 'Ladies and Gentlemen, we are privileged this evening to hear the immensely talented Miss Katy Lennox, who will entertain you in the break."

There was a spontaneous outbreak of applause which stopped Russ dead in his tracks. He listened as Katy began to play dance music, New Orleans style. The dance floor immediately filled up and Russ realised instantly that he had sold Miss Katy Lennox short. He joined his group outside for a joint of marijuana but he was restless as he could hear the swinging piano and the enthusiastic applause after each number. His drummer watched him and said, "Russ, that girl really swings."

"Yes, she does ... stub out that joint and let's join her and form a trio."

The pair went back in and Russ politely asked, "Katy would you mind if the drummer and I played some trad jazz with you?"

"Guys, I'd welcome it. It's hard work on my own."

Much to Katy's delight, Russ played her New Orleans tunes to perfection on the clarinet and the rapport of the trio was evident to the dancers who responded to that special tempo and wanted more when Katy's gig ended.

"This is a bit awkward, Katy," said Russ, "the crowd want you to stay on but I have to bring back my piano man."

"No worries, Russ, I'll play on as guitarist and banjoist ... no charge, mate. I'll do it for the love of it."

"Miss Lennox, you are a consummate professional and I apologise for my disdainful attitude earlier."

"Russ, you may call me Doll or Katy, anything you like. Let's keep the clientele on the floor dancing, even if the band plays pop stuff, OK?"

"But will you know the stuff we play, Katy?"

"Just hand me the score, Russ. I'm an excellent sight reader ... don't worry, I'll be fine."

Needless to say, the evening was an outstanding success which was repeated every evening for the duration of the voyage. Nifty doubled Katy's wages, on the condition that she kept that secret.

Russ and Katy spend most of their free time together in the mornings. Katy was becoming increasingly attracted to the new Russ, who treated her with a new-found respect, behaving impeccably well, despite Katy's inclinations to foster a closer relationship.

On the final night of the voyage, the band played and sang the appropriate farewell song ...

> *Here's to the next time and our merry greeting.*
> *Here's to the next time and our future meeting.*
> *Play it with rhythm, sing it in rhyme,*
> *Now, all together, here's to next time.*

As the musos packed their gear to tumultuous applause, a distinguished middle-aged lady approached Katy and handed her a business card. "My name is Linda Logan. My husband and I run a recording studio in Manhattan. If you are looking for work in New York, I'm sure we'll be able to help. I enjoyed your playing and hope to see you again soon."

So saying, she left, before Katy had a chance to read the card and respond.

Nifty joined Katy and said, "Well, lass, you've attracted the attention of a very influential New Yorker. I can't say I'm surprised ... you're going to have this world at your feet. Now, I normally invite the band to a little celebration in my cabin at this stage, before we go our separate ways. I hope you'll join us, Katy."

"Oh, Nifty, a team of wild horses couldn't keep me away. I've had a ball this trip."

"Righto, you hard-drinking boys, help yourselves to Jack Daniel's Kentucky bourbon. For our esteemed lady guest, I have the finest French champagne. Let me pour you a glass, Katy."

"I'm not a drinker, Nifty, but to be polite, I suppose I ought to sample French champagne, specially acquired for me. I feel privileged, and I'd like to toast the band who have made me feel so welcome."

Russ rose and said, "Fellas, I don't know about you, but I think we are the privileged ones."

The drummer responded, "Russ, you are so right. Katy is the best piano player I've heard since I recorded with Teddy Wilson. I lifts me lid to her … Cheers, Katy."

Katy's joy was unconfined as she savoured this unexpected compliment. It took her back to her days in Glasgow when she was introduced to the world of jazz. "That's nice to hear … it's my ambition to see Teddy Wilson in action. Have you any idea where he's appearing?"

The drummer said, "He's in New York, in one of the clubs on 42nd Street … I think it's the Two Deuces."

"Have another champagne, Katy," said Nifty. "Only you and I are drinking it, are you enjoying it?"

"I am, but I'm not used to alcohol. I guess another glass won't do me any harm."

Suddenly, the party was over, and the band headed back to their quarters below deck.

"Russ," said Katy, "I'm a wee bit unsteady on my feet. Would you be kind enough to walk me to my cabin?"

"Take my arm, Katy. I think that French wine has gone to your head."

On reaching her cabin, Katy said, "It's early, Russ, come in for a while and keep me company."

As soon as he entered, Katy kissed him passionately. "I don't want to be alone tonight, Russ. Come to bed."

"You're a bit tipsy, Katy. Are you sure you want to do this?"

"I've never been so certain of anything in my whole life."

Chapter 36

New York, New York, so good they named it twice.

Katy prepared for a lengthy stay,
Until she found herself in the family way.

She woke to lots of hustle and bustle, footsteps and voices passing her cabin. She turned, reaching for Russ, but she was alone. The ship had stopped. She rose and looked out the cabin porthole and saw the famous Manhattan skyline. A glance at the clock revealed that she had slept until 11am. As she showered, she reflected on the activities of the previous evening. She felt disappointment ... Russ had mounted her but shortly afterwards rolled off and fell asleep. She had likewise fallen asleep. Now, in the cold light of day, she thought, "What is all the fuss about? Is that all there is?"

Dressed and packed, she went in search of Nifty. "Ah, there you are, Katy. I was just about to come looking for you. Here's your wages, and exceptionally well earned. I hope you'll work for us again. You'll always be welcome."

"Well, when I've achieved what I came to America for, I'll take advantage of your offer and work my passage back to Blighty. By the way, have you seen Russ Lennox?"

"Oh, Russ left a couple of hours ago. He was rushing to catch a train to North Dakota."

"North Dakota ... that's a long way to go for a gig, isn't it, Nifty? Did he leave a message for me, by any chance?"

"Hardly, Katy, he has a wife and four kids up there. He is a crop duster pilot in the season and only comes to New York when things quieten down on the prairies."

Katy burst out laughing, causing Nifty to look at her questioningly. "It strikes me as being funny, Nifty ... a sophisticated musician in the city and a bit of a cowboy in the country."

"Oh well, a guy's gotta do what a guy's gotta do. Kids are expensive you know."

Katy nodded agreement and reflected that she had just learned her first lesson from an American. She realised that her infatuation for Mr Lennox had already evaporated and she was ready to get on with her real life. "I'll be needing a reasonably -priced hotel in New York ... any suggestions?"

"Yes, Katy, you can crash at a Cunard-owned apartment I share with my partner."

"Oh Nifty, she may not approve of another woman in the house."

"That won't be a problem. My partner is a man ... yes, Katy, I am queer. I thought you would have noticed that."

"No, I didn't, Nifty. I take people on face value and you have been a great friend to me from day one. I'll be delighted to take up your offer, and look forward to meeting your partner."

"Hi, Katy Lennox. I'm Charlie Baker. "Neville tells me you are a trad jazz fan, so you and I should gel just fine. Welcome to Chez Cunard."

"Thanks, Charlie, it's always good to meet a fellow jazz fan. Have you heard of Teddy Wilson, by any chance? He's been my idol for ages."

"Who hasn't, Katy? I have all the Benny Goodman Trio records."

"I'm really anxious to see Teddy Wilson in the flesh. I'm told he's at the Two Deuces ... do you know it, Charlie?"

"I sure do, Katy. Let's go there tonight."

"Well, that was quick ... how about you, Neville, are you in?"

"Knowing Charlie, I'd bet he's been living on junk food. I think I'll stock up and have something healthy to eat tomorrow. You two grab a cab and have fun. Look after her, Charlie ... she's a very special lady."

As the cab pulled up at the Two Deuces, Katy said, "I'm curious, Charlie, why would Neville tell you to look after me? Am I in some sort of danger here?"

"Not necessarily, Katy. Look, Nev calls me the Karate Kid. I have a black belt in karate. I've had to protect him in the past from prejudiced straight guys. You're a good-looking girl, Katy. Nev is probably worried that some Casanova may come on to you and give you a hard time tonight, OK?"

"OK, Charlie, let's get inside and see my idol."

The evening realised Katy's long-held ambition to be in the presence of the great Teddy Wilson and to hear him and his trio play the old Benny Goodman numbers. At the end of the session, she approached her idol, thanked him for his superb playing, and purchased a copy of his latest long-playing record, which he signed at her request.

"What a great night, Charlie, don't you agree?"

"The music was so good, Katy," said Charlie, "that I didn't have to threaten a single soul with violence."

"You're a funny guy, Charlie. Thank you for esquiring me tonight though ... I probably would have been a wee bit nervous on my own in the dark. Tomorrow morning, I'll be OK on my own. I'll take a cab to Mecca studios in Manhattan. I have a chance of a paying job there."

By mid-morning, Katy was greeted by Linda Logan. "Welcome, Katy Lennox ... have you found a decent place to live yet?"

"Yes, Linda, I'm with a friend on the Upper West Side but I haven't found a job yet."

"Katy, there are more musicians in New York than there are in the rest of America. Competition for work is fierce. You'll need an agent to find those jobs."

"Well, your card tells me you are a musician's agent, so can you take me on, Linda?"

"With pleasure ... with your talent, I guarantee we'll have a mutually profitable arrangement."

Over the following two months, Katy was working night and day, thanks to her talent and also to Linda's connections in the music industry. Charlie proved to be a great friend, collecting her from her late-night gigs. She was getting a great insight into the jazz scene in New York but was disappointed that bebop was beginning to hold sway at the expense of the trad musos. Her bank balance was decidedly healthy and, when she deemed that she had enough money, she intended to head for New Orleans to hear the real jazz which she preferred.

However, as they say, life happens when you're planning something else. Katy had missed two menstrual periods and a doctor confirmed that she was pregnant. She was devastated and could hardly believe her misfortune. God Almighty, one brief unsatisfactory coupling had presented her with a problem which she could well have done without. Charlie sensed that she was disturbed, far from her normal cheery self.

"You can talk to me, Katy," said Charlie. "That's what friends are for. We're friends, aren't we? What gives, love?"

"Oh, Charlie, I've been stupid and got myself in the family way. Jesus, Charlie, I'm not the motherly type. I'm a travelling musician, for Christ's sake."

"If you really feel so strongly about this, love, there are doctors in New York who can fix that for you."

"Yes, Charlie, I realise that but I don't want to subject my body to some backyard butcher. No, my friend, I'll go home to Scotland and be guided by my mother. As soon as Nev gets back, I'll see if he can use my services to get me back to Britain."

"He'll jump at the chance, Katy. He loves you and will fit you in as soon as possible."

She gave notice to Linda Logan, explaining the circumstances. "That's bad luck, Katy. I think you're doing the right thing, seeking your mother's advice. When everything is sorted out, you know I'll have you back on the books in a heartbeat."

Chapter 37

Decisions, decisions

Following a surprise confession,
Kate cures Sarah of depression.

By the time she arrived back in London, Katy was over three months into her pregnancy. She had already decided that her mother would never have approved of abortion, so she decided to keep working as long as she could in London, to lessen the time her mother would have to look after her. She was welcomed by Humphrey Lyttelton, who was only too willing to have her on the payroll.

In her sixth month, she was beginning to show, and it was time to place herself in the care of her beloved mother.

"Hello, Mum, I decided to surprise you by arriving unannounced ... sorry."

"There's no need to apologise, Kate. You'll always be welcome here. You should know that, lass. Is everything all right? You look as if you've been eating too much white bread," said Jean, smiling broadly. "Come on, Kate, out with it. How far gone are you?"

"Six months ... Look, Mum, I've been really stupid and now I'm paying for it. I've come to you because you're the only person in the world who can give me the right advice."

"Kate, that's nice to hear but I can't really offer advice until I know what your problem is. I mean, pregnancy is not an illness. All going well, in another three months, you'll give birth to a baby. Personally, I'll look forward to that ... another wee addition to the clan."

"Well, Mum, the problem is that I have no maternal instincts. For me, motherhood will just be a damn nuisance. My life is music and I can't be carting a child all over the world. It wouldn't be practical ... can't you see that?"

"Yes, Kate, I hear you and I understand but, like many reluctant mothers, you may change your mind after the bairn is born."

"Not me, Mum ... my career is my life. You must accept that."

"We'll see. At least, Kate, I'm glad you didn't consider abortion."

"I knew, Mum, that you would not have approved of that. Besides, I have too much respect for my own body to have it butchered."

"That's good to hear, lass ... but what are your intentions and isn't there a father in the picture?"

"The father doesn't know anything about my dilemma. He's somewhere in the backwoods of North America and I'll never see him again. My plan is to have the baby adopted straightaway. I'm hoping that you can organise that, Mum, ... make sure that it goes to a good home."

Jean smiled benignly, "I can guarantee that request easily, Kate. I'll adopt the bairn myself ... keep it in the family."

"What!" exclaimed Kate. "Surely you can't be serious, Mum ... aren't you too old to take that on?"

"Oh, for God's sake, lass, you don't think I'm going to farm my own granddaughter out to complete strangers, do you? Of course not, she'll be a welcome addition to our family."

It was Kate's turn to laugh. "You've already decided my baby will be a girl. Do you have second sight, Mum?"

Jean smiled, "Not really, Kate, my imagination just took over. I was visualising Joe dandling the wee girl on his knee and singing her praises, as he used to do with you."

"Mum, do we have to tell the rest of the family of my condition right now? I'd be very embarrassed. Am I asking too much to keep it secret ... is it possible?

"I think that's a good idea. The others are busy and haven't visited me for ages. They keep in touch by telephone. Sarah is back at work but Alec tells me she is still depressed over her miscarriage and her inability to have any children. Knowing that you were pregnant would not help. So, take it easy, play the piano for your dad. He'll be delighted that you are here."

The following three months passed uneventfully. Kate had a dream run with no morning sickness or any outlandish food desires. As soon as she felt labour coming on, Joe took her to Bishopbriggs Hospital, where she gave birth quickly and painlessly.

Jean visited her every day, waiting for a sign that Kate had changed her mind and wanted to keep the baby. No such sign appeared and a week later, Joe took her home. Jean decided that enough time had elapsed and she asked Kate outright whether she still wanted the bairn adopted.

"Yes, Mum, I'm delighted that you and Joe are willing to take her. You do still want to do that, don't you?"

"Of course, Kate. The wee lassie must remain part of our family. I just had to be sure that you have no regrets."

"Mum, as soon as I'm fit to travel, I'll be on my way."

Jean rang Alec and Sarah and asked them to come over as soon as possible.

"Is something wrong, Mum?" asked Alec.

"Far from it ... Kate's here and we have a decision to make. I want you and Sarah to be involved."

An hour later, Sarah and Alec arrived. "OK, Mum," said Alec, "Here we are. Now, what's all the mystery about?"

"Kate is here. Come on up to her bedroom and say hello."

"Is she sick?" asked Alec.

"No, far from it, she's in perfect health."

As they entered the bedroom, Kate smiled happily. "How are you both? It's been ages since I've seen you."

Sarah could see the cot beside the bed and looked at Jean inquisitively.

"Kate has given birth to a wee lassie," said Jean. So saying, she lifted the baby from the cot and handed her to Sarah. "Isn't she lovely, Sarah?"

Sarah walked round the room with the baby in her arms. As she turned towards Jean, she said, "She is the most beautiful baby I've ever seen. You're a very lucky girl, Kate." Her eyes welled up with tears as she reluctantly handed the baby back to Jean.

"Oh, Sarah, hasn't Mum told you? I'm not cut out for motherhood. I made one mistake in America and got myself pregnant, but I have no maternal instincts whatsoever. I just want to resume my career and carting a baby all over the world wouldn't be proper. I was going to put her up for adoption but Mum wanted her to stay in the family and volunteered to keep her."

Jean said, "You were concerned that I was too old to bring up another bairn, Kate and you may be right. Have you anything to say to Sarah?"

Kate gazed at Sarah, who was still sobbing quietly. "Sarah, I'd love it if you and Alec took the bairn. After all, she would still be in our family. Will you do that for me?"

Sarah nodded, too overcome with emotion to speak. Alec put an arm round her and said, "Kate, it will be our privilege and we accept wholeheartedly."

"Excellent," said Jean, "Take the bairn and the cot home with you tonight.

Kate isn't breastfeeding. I'll give you lots of formula based on soylac. When Kate was a bairn she was allergic to cow's milk but thrived on soylac. Right, off ye go and enjoy your new bairn. I'll ring you tomorrow to clear up a few minor details."

The following day, Kate announced that she was now ready to go.

"Well, Kate, all's well that ends well. Go forth and live life to the full in your chosen career. You've given joy to your big brother and his wife and, for that, I thank you."

As soon as Kate left, Jean rang Alec. "Hello, Alec, Kate has gone. We probably won't see her again for a few years but she is mistress of her destiny and if she's happy, I'm happy. How is Sarah getting on with her new bairn?"

"Oh, Mum, the baby cried through the night but Sarah was happy to stay up and nurse her. Her depression has gone completely."

"That's great, Alec. Now, I'm going to ask you and Sarah to break the law."

"Break the law? What are you talking about, Mum?"

"The baby's birth hasn't been registered. It will save a lot of trouble and extra paperwork if you register the bairn with you as the father and Sarah as the mother.

You'll have to choose a name for the bairn of course."

"That won't be a problem. Sarah had already chosen a name for the baby she miscarried. We will call her after Sarah's mother, so the wee lass will be Louisa MacDonald. I don't regard that as a criminal act and Sarah wouldn't care. This bairn has given my wife a new lease of life and she would fight tooth and nail to keep her. The birth certificate you propose eliminates any worry on that score."

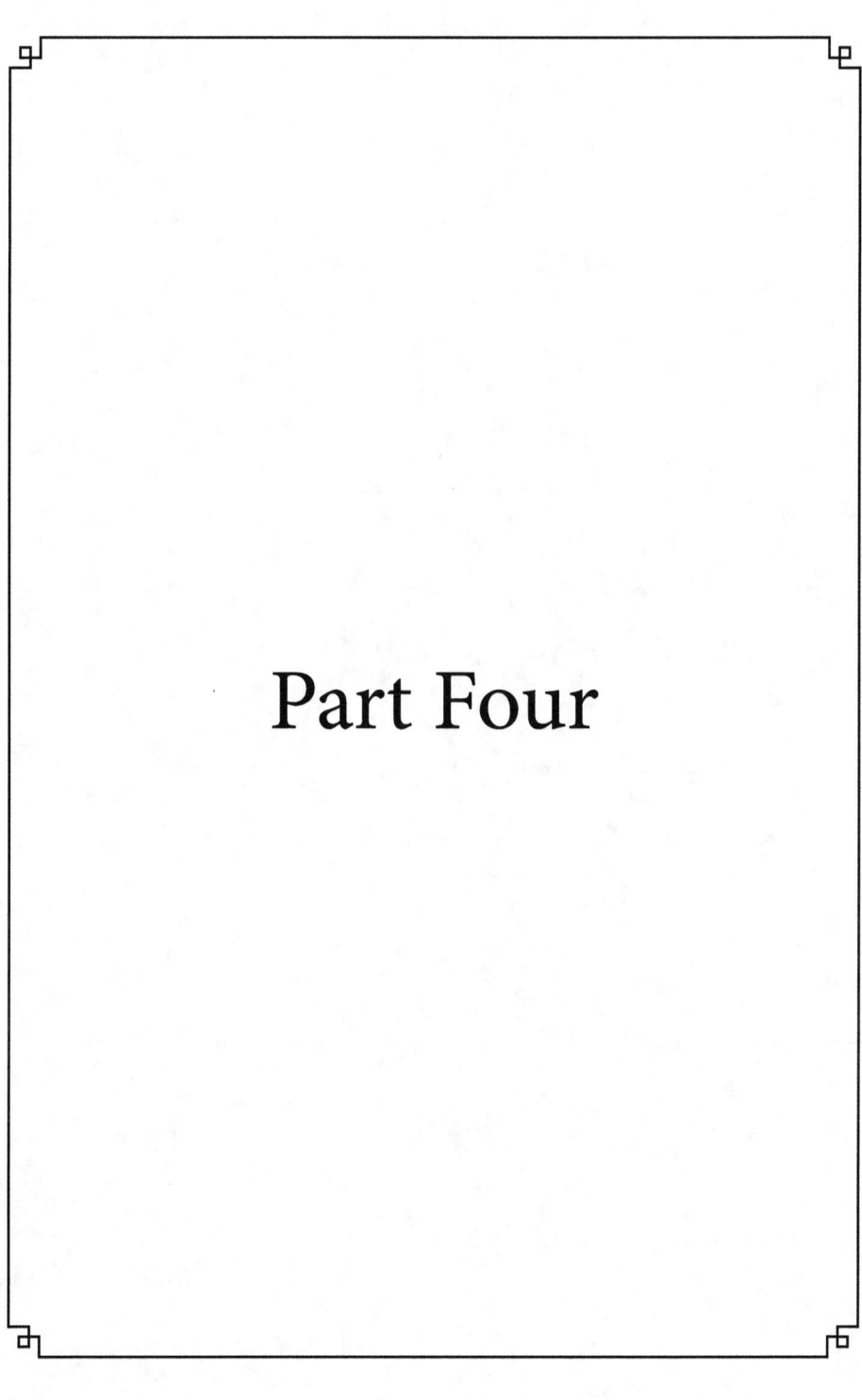

Part Four

Chapter 38

Hope Cowan

Hope starts her formal education;
The culinary arts prove her salvation.

$\mathcal{W}$ee Hope, who, as a seven-year-old had announced her ambition to be a 'cooker' just like her nana, left school when she was 14 years of age. Grace had long realised that her daughter was never cut out to be an academic. That didn't worry her as Hope was strong-willed and would doubtless find a job quickly. It came as no surprise when she started work as a kitchen maid in a local restaurant. Jem congratulated her and said she could learn a lot if she kept her eyes and ears open. His words came true as Hope graduated in the following two years from washing dishes to assisting the sous chef in the preparation of food. She proudly handed over the bulk of her meagre wages each week to her mother, to pay her way, as she put it.

On her 16th birthday, Jem asked her if her interest in cooking was as strong as ever.

"Dad, it's what I want to do. My employer is delighted at my progress but tells me that, at my age, some formal training would be necessary to achieve my ambition to become a chef."

"Well, Hope, it happens that I have had dealings with Isobel Gibson, who is the head of Domestic Science at Queen's College, in Glasgow. I've been telling her about you and, although you are a trifle young, she can enrol you in a 3-year diploma course in which you will learn all aspects of cooking."

"That sounds great, Dad, but I wouldn't be able to pay my way."

"Don't worry about that, Hope. Your mum and I will be only too happy to help."

Fiercely independent, Hope arranged to work weekends at the restaurant and thus could still contribute to the family finances.

Chapter 39

Katy finds her land of dreams,
Way down yonder in New Orleans.

On leaving Scotland, Kate felt the exhilaration of being free from an untenable situation while, at the same time, making Sarah happy. She drove to London and contacted Nifty to fix up another trip to America. Nifty was delighted and organised a drummer and bass player to form the Katy Lennox Trio on the Mauretania. On arrival in New York, Nifty paid her a huge bonus. "I'm heading straight for New Orleans, right away, Nifty, but I'll doubtless be contacting you when I want to get back to dear old Blighty."

"Oh, Charlie will be disappointed that you won't be staying in our unit, Katy."

"Give him my regards, Nifty. I'll look him up when I've had my fill of New Orleans."

"Oh, Katy, my biggest fear is that you'll fall in love with the town where jazz was born and, when they hear you play, they'll never let you go."

"I doubt that, Nifty, but hope springs eternal. I'd like to be appreciated there. We shall see."

"OK, Katy, I can see that you're determined to go ahead with this, so I suggest that you book into the Hotel Monteleone in the Vieux Carré, that's the Old French Quarter. It's right in the heart of the jazz scene and you can walk down Bourbon Street and listen to the jazz come out from each joint as you pass by.

As soon as Kate arrived in the Quarter, she was entranced by the aura of the place. It was quite unexpected but she soon learned that the environment was basically French. She read about the Louisiana Purchase, in which the state was bought from France and, to the present time, retained the atmosphere, due to the design of the buildings and the Creole population, who spoke a form of the French language.

The New Orleans brand of jazz was everywhere and she absorbed it joyfully as she strolled all around the city named the land of dreams. Bourbon Street was packed with tourists and on her third night, the hot climate had tired her and she decided to have an early night back at the Monteleone. The manager there saw that she was a bit frazzled and suggested that she visit the rooftop where a pool was available to cool off. As she sat on the edge and dipped her legs in the pool with no one else around, she was surprised when a group arrived and, in an adjoining room, set up their instruments and tuned up. On the stroke of 9 o'clock, the music started and an audience arrived to eat, drink and listen to the jazz. Kate heard enough to realise this was the best band she'd heard since arriving. Her fatigue vanished and she put on her shoes and entered the room. She sat down and saw that the band was named The Original Dixielanders. She ordered a cool drink and a snack and settled down to enjoy the music. The classic front line of cornet, clarinet, and trombone was backed by bass fiddle, banjo, and drums. There was no pianist but there was an upright piano, which was obviously a permanent fixture of the room.

As she listened to the old tunes with which she was familiar, she was itching to sit at that piano. She managed to restrain herself, closed her eyes and drank in the glorious New Orleans sound. However, when the band broke off for a drink and a smoke, she strolled over to the piano and quietly played 'Old-fashioned Love'. There was a ripple of applause and Kate launched into a rousing version of 'Maple Leaf Rag'. There were enthusiastic calls for more, but the band returned and Kate rose to return to her seat. The leader shook his head and pointed to the piano. "Sit in, girlie. The people like your stuff and so do I. We'll get round to introductions later."

At the end of the evening, she was formally established as a member of the Original Dixielanders and made the Monteleone as her base for the duration of her time in New Orleans. This was affordable as management, realising very quickly that she was bringing business to the hotel, cut her room tariff by half.

Two years later, she felt the urge to return to London to form her own small group and play swing music in addition to the Dixieland variety. She also had a foreboding about the health of her beloved dad and felt that she should be closer to him.

A week spent with Charlie in New York preceded the Mauretania gig which paid her way to the UK. Humphrey Lyttelton helped to install her in a flat in London and welcomed her back to his band. As in the past, Humph encouraged her to play a different kind of jazz in a trio or quartet, provided she kept herself available for his New Orleans group when necessary.

Kate had abandoned the idea of an all-girls band. Instead, she had no trouble picking up a male drummer, bassist, and clarinet player, all experienced musicians, only too happy to play in the Katy Lennox Quartet. Now, she had enough gigs to make a very comfortable living in the Greater London area, enjoying the profession she realised that she was born for.

Chapter 40

Hope chases Cordon Bleu accreditation,
The blue ribbon of her education.

*I*sobel Gibson took a special interest in Hope because of her youth but, after a short time, it was evident that the youngster did not need any extra tutelage. The girl's enthusiasm for the subject was nothing short of fanaticism, a fierce desire to succeed.

The years spent in the Lennox kitchen, learning the secrets of Jean's cooking, had given her a head start over the other first year pupils at Queen's College. Her weekend work at the local restaurant was also a current source of learning, and she had assumed the role of sous-chef before she was midway through her college course.

At the end of the three-year course, it came as no surprise to Isobel Gibson that her star pupil graduated top of her group with a first-class honours Queen's College diploma. "Congratulations, Hope, you've put in all the hard yards and deserve all the accolades which will come your way."

"To be perfectly frank, Isobel, I did not find the work hard at all. My time here has simply been a period of great enjoyment."

"Well, Hope, I can only say that you are a lucky member of a select group, having found your niche in life. The world is at your feet. Now, what are your plans for the future?"

"You'll probably laugh, Isobel, but I have this strange ambition to be a chef in the Houses of Parliament."

"Well, I'm not laughing, merely surprised, Hope. I'm curious how that idea came about."

"I remember the quiet pride of Jean Lennox after cooking for the big shots of the Co-op. They were all most complimentary of her tasty fare. Since then, I thought it would be great to cook for the blokes who run the country ... silly, isn't it?"

"Not at all, lass. You are aiming high and you are quite capable of doing it but the Civil Service fellows, who manage the day-to- day affairs at Westminster, insist on Cordon Bleu chefs."

"What does that mean, Isobel?"

"Oh, the arrogant Frenchies think they are the bees' knees and regard their Cordon Bleu diploma as the world's top award, the Blue Ribbon of cooking."

"Really? Well, how do I get one of those, Isobel?"

Isobel laughed at Hope's persistence. "Well, if you don't want to go to France, there's a Cordon Bleu College in London."

"Right ... that's where I'll go!"

"My God, Hope, there's just no stopping you, is there?"

"Well, Isobel, you know the old saying ... If you can't lick 'em, join 'em!"

"OK, as you are so determined, your Queen's College diploma plus a letter from me will get you in. I forecast that you'll be a Cordon Bleu chef within a year."

Hope was welcomed in London by Kate who had recently purchased a house in the suburb of Richmond upon Thames. Kate had lost the wander bug and realised that her musical life could be fulfilled in the Greater London area. She had more gigs than she could handle and more money than she'd ever had. She decided to invest in bricks and mortar in a classy environment, putting down a hefty deposit, leaving a mortgage with monthly repayments which her income could easily handle. A secondary investment in a car was required to transport her safely to and from gigs which usually did not finish until the small hours of the morning. The car would also ensure fast transport to Glasgow if her foreboding about her beloved dad came to fruition.

Hope lost no time in enrolling in the Cordon Bleu College and, still fiercely independent, secured a well-paid weekend job as cook in a city restaurant, so that she could pay her way at Kate's place. This worked out well as Hope did all the cooking, ensuring that Kate would have a nourishing meal after each gig. Although the pair did not see much of each other, Kate loved the arrangement and the friendly Glasgow accent when they did find time to be together. On one of these infrequent occasions, Kate asked Hope if she liked music.

"Oh, Kate, I was brought up listening to my mum playing piano. She played so beautifully ... how could I not like music?"

"Well, you always seemed so obsessed by helping my mum in the kitchen. I'm delighted that you enjoyed your mum playing. Do you remember this one?"

Kate played the introductory verse to 'These Foolish Things' and got the shock of her life when Hope sang the chorus in a contralto voice, in perfect pitch, with the emotion which the composer had obviously intended. "Hope, that was perfect. Why did we never know that you had this talent?"

Hope laughed. "Nana and I used to harmonise to my mum's piano and also yours, later on, while we were doing our own thing in the kitchen. I recall Nana saying that we had our own special talent, cooking ... let the others have theirs."

"To each his own," mused Kate, "My God, that mother of mine sure knew more than her prayers. However, now that I've heard you sing, Hope, you could perform with my band anytime you like."

"Thanks, but no thanks, Kate. Nana has the utmost faith that I could rise to the top of my profession and that's what I intend to do."

Isobel Gibson's forecast proved to be accurate as Hope was awarded the Cordon Bleu accreditation after 11 months. She lost no time in visiting Westminster and gained an interview with the appropriate civil servant. He read her resumé, perused her written qualifications at length, before saying, "Miss Cowan, I'm impressed that you've achieved all this at the age of 20. I offer you my sincere congratulations. However, we have no vacancies for someone of your qualifications at present. Nevertheless, I'll put you on file and contact you if an opportunity arises. I can tell you, though, that your chance of acceptance here will be enhanced when you attain the magic age of 21. In the meantime, I'm sure you will have no trouble finding alternative employment."

Although disappointed, Hope was not surprised. She told her present employer that she was now available for full-time work and her services were snapped up immediately. She told Kate, "I've been knocked back at Westminster. They reckon I'm too young."

"Oh well, that's their loss. What will you do now, Hope?"

"Well, I'm happy working full-time at the restaurant and very happy being here with you, Kate. I'll be 21 in a few months ... let's see what happens after that."

Three months later, glancing through the situation vacancies in the Times, her interest was aroused by an ad seeking a chef for the Ritz Hotel, Paris. Robert Spenser, at the London Cordon Bleu College was the man to ring. Hope decided to call in person as Robert had been her tutor at the college. She was ushered into his office without delay. "Well, well, young Hope Cowan, "said Robert, "I've missed you. Is this a social call?"

"No, Robert, I'm interested in the Paris Ritz job. I have a notion that a bit of experience in Paris may be useful, along with the Cordon Bleu diploma."

"It certainly won't do any harm, Hope. The head chef at the Ritz has asked me to interview applicants over here. They are getting more and more English-speaking guests there, mainly Americans. He has the reputation of being the finest chef in Europe. His name is Charles Lemont, but you will address him as Chef. Actually, you could be the person he's looking for. He wants someone young who will not be too arrogant to learn from him. You haven't asked me about remuneration, Hope ... normally that's the first thing people want to know."

"Robert, I'm ambitious, but not for money. I think it would be a privilege to serve with this man. I assume that my wage would be enough to keep the wolf from the door."

"It will, and there's a studio apartment, rent-free, so you won't have the hassle of finding a place to live in a very expensive city. You could learn a lot, Hope. Can I assume you're still interested?"

"Most certainly, Robert ... what happens now?"

"Well, the great man's decision will be final, but I shall forward your details, with the recommendation that you are the ideal applicant. I'll let you know his answer as soon as he responds. By the way, could you start right away?"

"Well, to be fair to my current employer, I'd have to give a week's notice."

"That's fine, Hope. You'll hear from me soon."

Chapter 41

Hope in Paris

The City of Light and the romantic aftermath
May lead Hope on a different path.

One week later, Hope had settled into an apartment which exceeded her expectations. She had met Charles Lemont and was pleasantly surprised to find that he wasn't a grumpy, demanding old fellow, like the other chef in London. Charles welcomed her, told her to enjoy her first weekend in Paris but be ready to start work on Monday at 8am. She was relieved that he spoke English as her knowledge of French was confined to menus and preparation of courses, learned at London Cordon Bleu College.

On Monday, in the heat of battle, as it were, she experienced another side of his character. During the morning, he had on several occasions yelled at her and demanded more speed. However, she kept her cool, following his instructions to the best of her ability. After the lunchtime rush, Charles beamed at her and said that she was going to be a great asset to his kitchen. "Tomorrow, you will be on the late shift,

Hope, gaining experience in our dinner menus. Today, I broke into my language on occasion, forgetting that you are English. I'm sorry about that."

"I understood what you needed, Chef, so that was no problem. By the way, I'm Scottish, not English, but I intend to learn your language as quickly as possible."

"Monsieur Spenser was right, Hope. You were the ideal applicant. I can see that you will be able to relieve me in the not-too-distant future."

A month later, Hope was really enjoying working as sous chef to the acknowledged best chef in Europe. The only snag in the ointment was that she was not progressing in learning French. On her time off, she was wandering the Paris streets, eavesdropping on conversations, but the locals spoke too fast and she was becoming frustrated. Returning to her studio apartment one afternoon, she was approached by a handsome young man. "My name is Harry Grant ... I'm your next-door neighbour. I'm glad I've bumped into you. I've seen you coming and going over the last few weeks, and thought it was high time we were introduced."

"You sound Scottish, although you talk pretty posh. My name is Hope Cowan and I hail from Bishopbriggs. I'm over here working at the Ritz Hotel."

"The Ritz is pretty posh, Hope. I teach at the International School, right here in the heart of Gay Paree. By the way, I was born and bred in Kilsyth, not too far away from Bishopbriggs. My parents were killed in a car accident but my only sister still lives in our parental home. It's a small world, Hope."

"I'm a chef by trade, Harry, and I'm here to gain experience in the ways of the French. I'd also like to learn the language but so far conversations between locals are unintelligible. The only French I understand is on Cordon Bleu menus. It looks like I shall have to do a correspondence course or go to night school."

"I may be able to help you with that, Hope. I teach French."

"Oh dear, Harry, I don't think I could afford you."

"Leave that for the moment, Hope. Have you visited many of the famous Paris attractions yet?"

"None whatsoever, Harry. I wouldn't know where to start, but why do you ask?"

"The best way forward for you to is to forget about doing a course in school French. You really want to be able to understand and converse in street French and where better to learn that but on the streets of Paris."

"But I've told you that I've tried that with no success."

"Oh, in another six months or so, you would improve but I could speed up your progress considerably at no expense to you."

"Harry, I don't know you. We've only just met. Why would you do that for me?"

"Oh, Hope, we're strangers in a strange land but we were practically neighbours in our homeland. We are fellow Scots. Why wouldn't I want to help you?"

"Well, I'm all ears, Harry."

"Firstly, let me squire you around the city. Wherever we go I shall speak to the natives slowly and ask them to respond accordingly. I'll translate to you as we go along. I guarantee you'll be surprised how quickly you'll catch on. You will surprise your workmates at the Ritz by your newly-found ability. In your free time, I'll monitor your progress but you'll really be teaching yourself, which is what the best education is all about. I learned school French at Kilsyth Academy but, like you, in France, I couldn't comprehend anything but a few phrases of the locals. It took me ages to learn street French on my own. I'm offering you what you need. The grammar may leave a lot to be desired but, what the hell, you're not sitting any exams."

"That's kind of you, Harry, and I accept your suggestions, but only if we go Dutch."

The following three months were a revelation to Hope. Harry took her to the Palace of Versailles, the Eiffel Tower, the Louvre Museum, Notre Dame Cathedral, and Le Moulin Rouge Restaurant, where Toulouse Lautrec used to sketch on the tablecloth.

Everywhere they went, Harry found people who obliged him by speaking slowly, waiting patiently while he translated to Hope. They tolerated Harry because he spoke perfect French, and they understood what he was trying to do. At each location, the conversation alluded strictly to its relevant peculiarities and history, making it easier for Hope to glean bits and pieces of the Parisian dialect. In addition, Harry decided to give her some formal education in the language, becoming aware that it was necessary in Hope's case if she was to pick up the street language quickly.

On her own, when Harry was not available, Hope persisted with her eavesdropping and found that many everyday phrases were becoming part of her French vocabulary. Indubitably, though, her greatest progress was at the Ritz, where the kitchen staff applauded her determination to learn and encouraged her to speak French all through her shifts. She was grateful to Harry but she was beginning to experience something beyond mere friendship. Although he had never made any untoward advances to her, she now instinctively sensed that he had similar feelings about her. This was completely new to her as she'd never been involved with men apart from those with a mutual interest in cooking. Subsequently, she began to take more interest in her appearance, spending time at the hairdresser, being coiffured, taking advice about styling from the expert, who obviously was aware that Hope was trying to impress some man.

Three months later, Hope began to think that she had been mistaken in thinking that Harry had feelings for her. He pecked her chastely on the cheek each time that he saw her to her door after the customary evenings of street learning. However, he didn't seem to regard their times together as a chore. He was highly entertaining and they laughed and joked a lot.

Ultimately, Hope, now hopelessly infatuated with him, said in frustration,

"Harry, after all the times we've been together, you've always said goodnight with a peck on the cheek. Have you never felt like bidding me goodnight with a kiss on the mouth?"

Harry stared at her for what seemed an eternity before replying, "Hope, if I kissed you on the mouth, I wouldn't want to say goodnight."

"Oh, Harry, did it never occur to you that I may not want you to say goodnight?"

"No, Hope, I always thought that you regarded me more like a big brother."

"Well, let's put it to the test, shall we?"

She puckered up and kissed him, whereupon he grasped her firmly and the chaste kiss developed into a passionate union. Hope gasped and managed to whisper, "Come inside, Harry."

One year later, although retaining their separate apartments, the couple were virtually living together in a genuine love match. Hope, although still passionate about her career, would have conceded, if asked, that paté de fois gras was not as important now as it had been before she discovered the thrill of sexual love. Nevertheless, she was also ecstatic about her command of the Parisian street language, for which she was indebted to Harry Grant, the love of her life.

Chapter 42

Harry determines to propose,
Now his tenure's at a close.

"Hope, my contract at the International School is coming to an end shortly," said Harry, "and I'll be heading back to Scotland. You know that I love you, don't you?"

"I think you've proved that, Harry, and I love you too. What's on your mind, sweetheart? You're not your usual cheerful self. Should I be worried? Are you telling me I'm never going to see you again?"

Harry smiled reassuringly, "Au contraire, mon amour. I'm trying, in my clumsy way, to propose marriage. Do you accept, my love?"

Hope came into his arms and kissed him. "I do, darling, wholeheartedly, but I want to be married in Scotland. I don't want a big wedding … We'll be married quietly at the registry office on our own but, as soon as I can assemble the clan, we'll have a belated reception in Bishopbriggs."

"That's fine, Hope. I took the liberty of buying an engagement ring and trust you'll like it."

"Of course I'll like it." She put it on, declaring, "Wonderful, we are now officially engaged. When you leave for the old country, I shall miss you dreadfully, but when you find a job and are settled, I will give notice to the Ritz and come back home."

The following few weeks seemed to fly by as their love was well and truly consolidated. On the morning of his departure, Harry urged her to keep up her French language education. "You've done really well, Hope, having achieved more than you expected or even needed. However, don't stop, darling. Learn ten or so new words of vocabulary every day."

"OK, Harry, I will, although when we are married and living in Scotland, I'll probably never speak French again."

"Ah, but you will, Hope. As a French teacher, my summer holidays were always spent in France. In the future, we'll travel together to different regions of the French countryside, and you'll enjoy the experiences much more, the more fluent you become."

With Harry gone, Hope assuaged her loneliness by studying harder than ever. She joined a local library and explained to the librarian her need to find simple stories to enlarge her vocabulary. The librarian was most helpful, providing novellas written with a market of young adults in mind.

A month later, Harry wrote with good news. He has a job, and will be teaching French at Kilsyth Academy, his old school, next term. Furthermore, he has taken over the mortgage payments on his sister's house, as she is about to emigrate to Australia with her fiancé. "I'm sure you will like the house, Hope. It is on the hill overlooking the town and, on a clear day, you can see the county of Lanarkshire spread out below. Come over as soon as you can … I'm missing you more than words can say."

Chapter 43

For Harry only, Hope does yearn,
Her career no longer her main concern.

*I*n deference to Charles Lemont, who had taught her so much, she offered to work out a month's notice. "Oh, Hope, I thought you were happy here ... I'm disappointed that you have decided to leave."

"I have been happy here and grateful to you for your patience with me. I am going back to Scotland to get married. My husband-to-be has bought a house and awaits my arrival."

"I see," said Charles, "well, in that case, far be it from me to stand in the way of young love. One week's notice will suffice, Hope, and I wish you every happiness."

Harry met Hope at Glasgow Central railway station and they drove straight to Kilsyth as Hope couldn't wait to see her new residence and Harry was impatient to renew their long-awaited intimacy.

Following a night of love, Harry said that he had already been in touch with the Glasgow Registry office and they could be married the next day. Hope immediately rang her mum. "I'm back in Scotland, Mum, with my fiancé, Harry Grant. If you and Dad are free tomorrow, we can pick you up and take you to be witnesses at our wedding in Glasgow. Will you both be available?"

"Of course we will, Hope. My God, you sure are full of surprises. Welcome back to Bonny Scotland. I'm looking forward to meeting Harry."

"Good, Mum, I'll have a lot to tell you but I know that you and Dad will like my choice of husband. OK, I must go, lots to do, will see you at eleven tomorrow."

At the allotted time next day, Grace was delighted to see that Harry was so handsome and Jem was gratified to find that Harry was an experienced schoolteacher. Hope's parents, on the drive to Glasgow, were pleased to discover that their daughter had found a quiet, polite young gentleman, and they nodded their approval to each other in the back seat of the car. Their joy was unconfined when Hope told them that Harry had taken over the payments on the parental house in Kilsyth and would be teaching at Kilsyth Academy next term.

Following the simple marriage ceremony, they went back to Bishopbriggs and Hope told her parents the entire history of the relationship, starting in Paris.

"Now that you are married, with a good man to look after," said Grace, "will you be giving up the profession you were crazy about?"

At that juncture, Harry intervened, "Oh, Mrs Cowan, I have no wish to make any such demands on Hope. We haven't really discussed her future but she, and she alone, will decide what she wants to do. I'm well aware how strong-willed she is. By the way, do you know that she speaks French like a native?"

"Oh, Mum, Harry is a French teacher and he encouraged me to learn conversational French but he is a wee bit prone to exaggeration about my talents."

"Well, Harry Grant, you've ticked all the boxes, and Jem and I welcome you wholeheartedly into our family. Now, you are too mature to call us Mum and Dad, so please from now on, address us as Grace and Jem. Now, Hope, my stomach thinks my throat has been cut, so how about you cooking up a bit of lunch?"

While Hope prepared a simple meal, she took her time, allowing her parents to really get to know the man she adored.

"Well, Hope, that was a lovely meal," said Grace, "you haven't lost your touch. I suppose you two want to go on your honeymoon now, so don't let us keep you."

"Yes, Mum, we'll have our honeymoon in our house in Kilsyth but I want to see Nana and Gramps first. She was my first mentor in the cooking business. I love her and I want to show off my new husband. You'll be seeing us often from now on. I'm never going to leave again. You know, Mum, I never felt homesick for Scotland until I was on the train coming up from London. Isn't that strange? I think that I've been so single-minded about my career that I never had time to miss my homeland. That's all changed now ... I have a new life ahead with Harry. I'll still work but I won't be obsessed like before."

Chapter 44

Harry and the Lennox pair
Find a history which they share

"Nana, meet my brand-new husband, Harry Grant. Harry, this lady is Jean Lennox, my first cooking mentor."

"Well, this is a pleasant surprise," said Jean. "I'm very pleased to meet you, Harry. Truth to tell, I'm absolutely delighted. I thought that Hope was destined to stay married to the kitchen."

"And I'm so happy to meet you, Mrs Lennox, and it …"

"Oh, please call me Jean, Harry, and call my husband Joe … I'm sorry to interrupt you. Now, please finish what you were about to say."

"I was just going to say that it took me a long time to convince Hope that there was another world outside the kitchen."

"Where's Gramps, Nana?" said Hope.

"Oh, he's pottering about in the garden. Fetch him in, Hope, while I put the kettle on."

Hope found Gramps dozing on the garden seat. She shook him gently and told him that he was about to meet the man in her life. She took his arm and led him into the living room. "Harry, this gentleman is Joe Lennox. Gramps, meet my husband, Harry Grant."

"A fine Scottish name, Harry, welcome to the clan. I'm presuming that you are Scottish."

"Thanks for the welcome, Joe. Yes, I was born and bred in the best country in the world, not too far from here, actually."

"I'm getting old and a wee bit tired, Harry, but that accent I could never mistake. I'd say you are a Kilsyth boy."

"That's amazing, Joe, as I left Kilsyth a long time ago and have been living in France, where I met Hope."

"Ah, Harry, you can take the boy out of Kilsyth but you can't take Kilsyth out of the boy. I should know, as Jean and I were originally from Kilsyth. I used to have a shop there, selling foodstuff. Incidentally, I had a part-time employee named Harry Grant. He was a schoolboy who used to come in and stock the shelves before school. After school, he'd do some deliveries for me on his bike. He lived in Shuttle Street. Could he have been related to you?"

"I can't believe this ... this amazing. That was my dad ... you wouldn't be Papa Joe Lennox, by any chance?"

Joe smiled, "Yes, I was called that ... the shop was named Papa Joe's."

"Well, Joe, when I was little more than a toddler, I heard my granny talking about you and how you helped people in the hard times, including her. I'm privileged to meet you, a legend in my home town."

"I remember your dad for a particular reason," said Joe. "His father was a coal miner on strike. Young Harry wouldn't take cash from me. He just wanted groceries to help put food on the table. I admired him for that. He was only 12 then. Do your folks still live in Shuttle Street, Harry?"

"No, Joe, I'm the sole survivor of the Grant family but Hope assures me that I have plenty of relatives now."

"Yes, that's true, Harry," said Joe. "You come from good stock and I'm the one who is privileged to include you in our extended family."

Chapter 45

1965

Katy Lennox is singing the blues,
Dreading the approach of real bad news.

Kate received a letter from Hope, telling her she was back in Scotland, married, and living in Kilsyth. Hope gave her details of the address and said she was welcome there any time just as she had been welcomed in Richmond. The letter was short, with no news about the rest of the family. Kate surmised that no news was good news and felt confident enough to get on with her busy life, doing as many gigs as she could handle and saving heaps of money. She found time to indulge in a few brief affairs and, although she hadn't fallen head over heels in love, she was relieved and pleased to discover that sex could be really satisfying, unlike the experience with Russ Lennox on the Mauretania. However, she'd learned that contraceptives should be used on every conceivable occasion ... no more motherhood for her.

However, two months later, that nagging premonition reappeared and she decided not to wait for bad news but to drive to Scotland as soon as she organised a replacement for her in the quartet. Humphrey Lyttelton arranged everything for her and asked when she'd be coming back.

"I really don't know, Humph. This is a family problem which I have to attend to but I've no idea how long it's going to take."

"OK, Katy, I understand, but you'll be missed. Let's hope you get back to us soon."

Kate drove to Carlisle and stopped there overnight, too tired to go all the way. At dawn, she drove on and reached Hope's house in Kilsyth around noon.

"Kate, I've been ringing you every hour. Obviously, someone else has told you the news."

"Nobody has told me anything, Hope. I just felt that something bad has happened to my father. What is it?"

"Joe Lennox has had a heart attack and is in the Royal Infirmary."

"Right, I'll get in there now."

"Good, Kate, I saw Joe yesterday with my mum and dad but I'll come with you. We can have a talk on the way."

On arrival at the Royal, Joe was awake and able to talk, although he looked very pale. Jean was by his side but she and Hope left the room to give Kate a chance to talk to her beloved dad. "Ah, Kate, I'm glad you came up from London. It's been about thirteen years since I last saw you but I've been following your career and am very proud of you."

"Dad, have the doctors treated you yet?"

"Well, Kate, they've done lots of tests. It appears that I have a partially blocked heart artery and when I overdo things, like gardening, I'm liable to pass out."

"Can they fix it, Dad?"

"Not really, love. It's too dangerous to try to operate. Complete rest is what they recommend. They will send me home tomorrow with strict instructions to take it easy ... no strenuous gardening, or the like."

"Oh, Jesus, Dad, that'll be hard for you. You've always been active."

"That's true. Listen, Kate, I've exceeded the three score and ten, and I feel that my quality of life isn't going to be up to much. Your mother understands ... she wouldn't want me to live like a damn vegetable. She accepts the situation calmly, like the strong woman she has always been. Now, you're of the same mould, Kate, so I'll tell you what I've told her. When I go, I don't want a big fuss ... just a family affair. Try to celebrate the time we've had as a group, quite a big group, an extended family. Can you promise me that you'll support your mother in this?"

"I will, Dad, I promise."

"I need a wee sleep now, lassie. I'll see you at home tomorrow."

Kate gazed at her adopted father, the man whose surname she had chosen for herself, so high in her esteem was this prince among men, who'd achieved so much and shared the bounty with so many other people. Now, she saw him, sleeping like a young child and she thought that Joe Lennox would never suffer the ignominy of a second childhood. No, he would bypass that phase of human life and this latest premonition was one which she would welcome, in full knowledge that her dad would be in total agreement.

"Mum, Dad's asleep now," said Kate. "As he is going home tomorrow, I'll see you there."

"That's fine, Kate. Jim will be there. He'll be on his way from Inverness in the morning. Joe wants to see his immediate family tomorrow so Alec will be there too. I'll stay here until Joe wakens up."

"OK, we'll be off then," said Kate. "I'll get Hope home now and meet her new husband."

As they drove to Kilsyth, Kate said, "I don't know why my dad wants to see only his immediate family tomorrow, Hope. That seems a wee bit strange, don't you think?"

"No, Kate, I think that's only natural. It's been a long time since he's had you all together. Anyway, you'll find out tomorrow what he has in mind. In the meantime, would you mind taking me to Queen's College. I just want a quick word with my old mentor, Isobel Gibson?"

"No problem, Hope, take all the time you need."

"Isobel, can you spare a few minutes to talk to a former pupil?"

"Hope Cowan, home on holiday, are you?"

"No, I'm home for good, Isobel. I'll never live anywhere else but Scotland from now on."

"What happened to your ambition to cook for those MPs in Westminster?"

"Oh, the Civil Service turned me down, even though I had a Cordon Bleu. They thought I was too young. Anyway, I've been working at the Ritz in Paris, where I met my husband. He was teaching at the International School in Paris but now he has a job at Kilsyth Academy and we are living in Kilsyth."

"So, are you retired, Hope?"

"Oh no, far from it. I'll probably find a hotel job after we've settled in to our new house."

"How would you like a Monday to Friday, 9 to 4 job, so that you can spend more time with your man?"

"I'd love that, Isobel, but cooking jobs don't have regular hours and they usually have split shifts."

"We have a vacancy coming up shortly, Hope. The position is yours if you want it."

"Teaching? Oh Isobel, I don't think I'm qualified for that."

"You'll be an excellent teacher and you will enjoy it. Just imagine you are the head chef and you are demonstrating your skills to a group of young folk, all keen to learn, just as you were. You are a Cordon Bleu with a lot of experience. Are you in?"

"Well, Isobel, you make it sound attractive. As you have confidence in me, I accept gladly."

"Fine, Hope, the job will be yours in two weeks. We'll see you then."

"I'm sorry to keep you waiting so long, Kate, but I've just been offered a job and I'll be teaching at Queen's College in two weeks."

"That's wonderful, Hope ... now let's go, I'm dying to meet your Harry."

"Ah, you're home, darling. Meet my very good friend, Kate Lennox. Kate, this is my man, Harry Grant."

"Well, what an honour to meet the famous Katy Lennox. I've heard all about you. You are a legend."

"Yes, that's me, Harry, a legend in my own lunchroom. No, Harry, Joe Lennox is the real legend in our family. I just make a reasonable living playing jazz. Do you like that kind of music?"

"I sure do. When I was a schoolboy, I spent any pocket money buying a 78 record every month. Muggsy Spanier and Benny Goodman were my favourites. In Paris, I saw Louis Armstrong and Sidney Bechet, who lived there for a while. They were made welcome there. There is no racial prejudice in Paris, at least as far as music is concerned."

"I'm glad you're a jazz fan, Harry. I haven't recorded anything yet, although I've had a few offers from Decca. One of these days, I'll accept. Humphrey Lyttelton is always urging me to leave something for posterity."

"I'd love to hear you play," said Harry, "but we don't have a piano here."

"Would you settle for banjo or guitar, Harry? If so, after we gorge on Hope's cooked dinner, I'll take requests, OK?"

Hope was delighted that Harry and Kate were getting on like a house on fire. After dinner, the evening was a joyous concert, with Hope singing along to Kate's wonderful improvisations. Around midnight, Kate called a halt, "I'm worried about the neighbours, Hope."

"Oh, let them buy their own banjo," said Hope.

The happy trio laughed and retired for the night.

Next morning, after a leisurely breakfast, Kate left to attend the family meeting. However, she deviated and arrived at Alec and Sarah's house. "Hello, Sarah, long time no see. I thought I'd pick up Alec and take him to the family meeting.

"Alec is at work, Kate. He'll go to the meeting straight from work. I'm glad you're here, though. I'd like Louisa to meet you ... she's nearly 14 now. Louisa, come and say hello to your Aunt Kate."

"Hello, Aunt Kate, I've heard a lot about you and your piano playing."

"Hi, Louisa, I haven't seen you since you were a baby. Now, you are a beautiful young lady."

"Louisa is a musician too, Kate. She has been learning cello for over 5 years and will be starting a diploma course at the Scottish Academy of Music next year."

"That's wonderful, Louisa," said Kate. "I daresay you practise every day."

"I do, Aunt Kate. Gramps likes to hear me play. He likes to hear 'The Londonderry Air' on the cello. He told me that you played 'Moonlight Sonata' for him. I'm sure that is his favourite, so I've been practising it. Would you listen to my version and tell me if I've got it right?"

"I'd love to hear you play, Louisa."

As the girl played, Kate closed her eyes and allowed the music to transport her to a former world of classical music. Suddenly it was over, and Kate opened her eyes to see Louisa staring at her enquiringly. "Oh, Louisa, that was so beautiful. Your grandfather will love that. It was simply perfect. Perhaps you and I may play it together for him sometime soon. Do you intend to have a career in music?"

"Aye, I do, Aunt Kate. My ambition is to play in a symphony orchestra."

"Well, Louisa, from what I've heard today, I don't think you'll have any problem. Now, I must be off to see your gramps."

Sarah came outside to see Kate off. As Kate reached her car, Sarah said, "Tell me Kate, was Louise's father a musician?"

"Yes, Sarah, he was, and a very good musician at that."

"I'm not surprised," said Sarah. "In a few years, she'll be off, travelling with an orchestra. I've come to realise that we don't really own children. They own us but, when the time comes, they must make their own way. I've come to accept that, Kate, and am happy to look after her until then. Alec says that, when the time is right, the wee birdies have to leave the nest, or the big birdies will pick them to death. That's life."

"Your wee lassie is something special, Sarah. Just love her and enjoy her, even when she leaves the nest. She's lucky to have you as her mother."

Jean welcomed her three children as they arrived, within minutes of each other.

"Joe is asleep at the moment but he gave me strict instructions to wake him up, the moment you all arrived. OK, I'll get him up and he can have a chat to you while I prepare lunch."

Joe came into the living room, clad only in dressing gown and slippers. He hugged each of them in turn and they sat at the dining room table. "It's been a long time since we've been together and I want to take this chance to speak to you. Now, although we are not related by blood, I feel in my heart that we are family and have been ever since your mother consented to be my wife. As you can see, I'm not in good health and, even with all the rest I've been having, I'm getting steadily worse. If this heart valve blockage causes me to black out again, I don't want to be resuscitated.

My quality of life will not improve, so I ask you to support my request. Your mother has already pledged to grant my wish so, if the whole family is in agreement, there can be no argument from anyone else. Do you have any questions?"

"Would a second opinion be worthwhile?" said Jim.

"My GP and the specialists know that nothing can be done, Jim. The condition is inoperable. Now, are you all agreed?"

The three nodded at each other and Kate said, "Yes Dad, we'll do as you ask."

"Good, that's settled then. I just want you to know that I'm very proud of the three of you, and everything that each of you has achieved. Right, enough of that ... here comes your mum with the victuals."

Jean placed a simple salad on the table for each to help themselves. Joe said, "Jean, I don't feel like eating. Can you get me a drink?"

"Certainly, my love."

She rose from the table and brought back a bottle of 12yo malt whisky and poured a generous helping into a glass. "Oh, Mum, should Dad really be having that?" said Kate.

Joe smiled, "Ah, Kate, Kate, surely you wouldn't deny your dad the only pleasure he has left?"

Kate relaxed and said, "Drink up, Dad, enjoy every sip. You've earned it."

As Joe relished the fine malt, he said, "What a pity we don't have a piano here. I would have loved a tune or two, Kate."

"Well, as it happens, I have my guitar in the car ... I'll fetch it, shan't be a minute."

On her return, she began to play the soulful 'Danny Boy, the Londonderry Air'.

As Joe listened, the tears began and he held out his glass for a top up. When Kate played the last poignant notes, Joe said, "Well, Kate, you've made me cry, but they are tears of happiness. At this moment, I could go in perfect contentment." He got to his feet to propose a toast but dropped his glass and collapsed on the floor.

Jim immediately put his wartime medical training to work but, after checking the pulse and breathing said, "He's gone. He has his wish ... he's beyond resuscitation."

Kate began to weep but she said, "Thank God ... he won't suffer any more."

Jean was of course sad that her man was gone but she'd been expecting it and was relieved that he didn't have to persevere with a life not worth living. She rang an ambulance and assured the operators that there was no emergency as her husband was dead. She advised them to bring the coroner to confirm death and make the necessary arrangements.

Chapter 46

Denouement

A time of quiet contemplation
Followed by a double celebration

At the funeral chapel, there were fifteen mourners present. Jean had asked the Presbyterian minister to keep his speech short. The cleric complied and Jean thanked him for his words of consolation.

The best qualified person to deliver the eulogy was Jim MacDonald, the writer, poet, and English teacher. However, he had declined, fearful of having an emotional breakdown. He suggested that his early mentor, Jem Cowan, would be an ideal choice. Jean had agreed and at the chapel she invited Jem to speak.

"It is an honour and a privilege to deliver a eulogy in memory of Joe Lennox. In his home town, Kilsyth, he ran a grocer's shop called Papa Joe's, during the depression. He was never able to refuse credit to needy mothers unable to feed their bairns. Despite this, he still managed to keep his head above water. He is a legendary figure in Kilsyth and a substantial number of people he had helped repaid him when economic conditions improved. If this funeral was public, there would not be enough room in this chapel to accommodate the number of people who hold him in high regard. Since those dark days, Joe has become the patriarch of an extended family. Although, he is not related by blood to anyone here today, I can confidently state that every person present has, either directly or indirectly, benefited from his wise advice or financial assistance, and his love. He never pressured any of the recipients of his help, but expected them to try their best to achieve their personal goal. To each his own was a favourite saying. Personally, I benefited greatly from his largesse. I'll conclude by saying that his generosity knew no bounds. He was the finest man I have ever known. Vale, Joe Lennox."

The group made its way to the spacious home of Jem and Grace. Drinks and nibbles were available and when everybody was settled, Jean said, "At Joe's request, we're going to have a party but, before we let our hair down, we can have a time of quiet reflection while Kate and young Louisa play Joe's favourite piece, 'Moonlight Sonata'."

Kate played obligato to Louisa's melody on the cello. As Grace, no mean pianist herself, listened to Kate's improvisation of genius, she reflected that Beethoven would have approved. As Jean looked around, she saw that there was hardly a dry eye in the house. As the last poignant notes resounded, there was a spontaneous outburst of applause. Jean then said, "I think we are blessed to have such musical talent in our family. Before the fun gets under way, I'd like to introduce Harry Grant, the latest addition to the family. Harry, say a few words if you please."

Harry said, "I'm not much of a public speaker but, having married the lovely Hope, a Cordon Bleu chef, there is no danger of me suffering from malnutrition." He then sat down to gales of laughter and applause.

"Well said, Harry, short and sweet," said Jean, "now we shall have music and dancing, so let joy be unconfined. Feel free to raise the rafters."

Grace sat down at the piano and was joined by Kate, alternating between banjo and guitar. The keen dancers were soon on the floor, enjoying the swinging music. Hope joined the band to sing a couple of numbers before jiving with Harry, who proved to be a smooth operator as a jazz dancer.

Kate glanced at young Louisa and noticed that she was tapping her foot and clapping her hands to the jazz rhythm. She mused that the youngster may become hooked as she had been all those years ago. Sarah was dancing with Alec and looked happy but Kate wondered what her reaction would be if Louisa wanted to play jazz. Kate shook her head as she dismissed the thought and concentrated on the music.

Malcolm Cowan was keeping his dad company while his mum was playing piano. The young man was over the moon as he'd just been signed to a professional contract with Heart of Midlothian, a first division football club. Not for him, the academic world. He preferred outdoor work and had been keeping fit and building up his strength as a builder's labourer, while playing minor league football with Kilsyth Rangers. He was now 20 years old and had never had a regular girlfriend but he couldn't keep his eyes off a beautiful young lass at the other side of the room. He pointed her out and said, "Dad, please tell me that she's not a cousin I've never met."

Jem smiled, "No, Malcolm, she's no relation. That's young Jean Macdonald, the daughter of Jim Macdonald. You've never met her because she lives in Inverness. Why don't you go over and ask her to dance?"

Jean saw the tall, muscular young man approaching and felt a thrill of anticipation. She was almost 17 and had been chased by quite a few schoolboys but they had seemed immature to her. He stood before her, smiling. "Hello, Jean, I'm Malcolm Cowan, would you care to dance?"

"I'd love to," she said, "but I'm not a very good dancer."

"Neither am I," said Malcolm, "so we'll just walk around and I'll try not to step on your toes."

She felt as light as a feather in his arms and they acquitted themselves quite well. Soon, he felt confident enough to talk. "Are you still at school, Jean?"

"No, Malcolm, I'll shortly be starting a course in medicine at Edinburgh University."

He felt a surge of elation. "Well, at the start of the football season, I'll also be based in Edinburgh, playing for Hearts. Perhaps we can be friends and see each other, if you like."

"I'd like that very much. I can come and watch you play on Saturday sometimes."

The young couple were inseparable for the rest of the day.

The two musicians, after an hour or so, stopped for a rest. Sarah approached Kate and told her that Louise has been smitten by the jazz.

"I'm not surprised, Kate, considering her bloodlines. I really wouldn't mind if that's what she decides to do. To each his own, as Joe often said, but I'm hoping you can have a word with her and offer some advice."

"Yes, Sarah, I'll give her the same advice Joe gave me ... call her over."

Young Louise came over, wreathed in smiles. "Aunt Kate, I can't tell you how much I enjoyed your music. I'd love to be able to entertain people in the way you and Grace Cowan do."

"Well, Louise, Grace completed her classical education before taking up teaching. I obeyed the wishes of Joe Lennox to graduate from the Academy of music. Only then did I choose a different path. You may be surprised how many great jazz players were classically trained. Now, you are very talented but I think you ought to study cello and graduate with the highest degree. Then, if you still want to play jazz, you can switch to violin, double bass, guitar, or whatever takes your fancy."

"Thanks, Aunt, I am enjoying my study, so I'll do as you suggest. Maybe I can talk to you again in a few years. In the meantime, I'll collect some jazz recordings, just to hear the greats."

Sarah privately thanked Kate before joining Alec and Louisa. As Kate looked at them, she had a premonition that one day Louisa MacDonald would become an important part of the Katy Lennox Quintet.

Jean Lennox cast her eyes over the proceedings and was happy with what she saw.

She was now matriarch of this extended family but she knew that she could never replace Joe in the leadership he had shown all his life. She shared his compassion but not his wisdom or brilliance. As the celebrations drew to a close, she stood and begged the group's attention for a few minutes.

"Thank you all for coming today. I'm not going to dwell on the passing of Joe Lennox. Jem captured the essence of my husband in his thoughtful eulogy. His legacy will be the people here who benefited and learned from him. They will be able to guide their offspring in the right way so, in a way, Joe will always be with us. Before we go our separate ways, I'll borrow his mantra."

To each his own,
I've found my own,
Each and every one of you.